Sherlock Holmes
and the
Telephone Murder Mystery

John Hall

First published in 1998 by
Breese Books
This revised edition published in 2020 by
Baker Street Studios Ltd and
The Irregular Special Press for
Breese Books
Endeavour House
170 Woodland Road, Sawston
Cambridge, CB22 3DX, UK

ISBN: 978 0 947533 47 2

Cover Illustration: Retrograph Archive.

Typeset in 8/11/20pt Palatino

This book is dedicated to
all those who have ever visited
Mount Pleasant, Reigate,
a delightful place which
(it is perhaps unnecessary to add)
bears only a coincidental and passing resemblance
to the country house described here!

Dramatis Personae

At 221B Baker Street

Mr Sherlock Holmes
Dr John H Watson

The staff at Belmont

Gordon Morrison, secretary
Ernest Welsh, gardener and handyman
Mrs Welsh (Ernest's wife), housekeeper
Frederick Evans, assistant gardener
John Merryweather, assistant gardener

The guests at Belmont

James Davenport, engraver
Peter Gregson, sculptor
Jeremy Lane, writer
Benjamin Morgan, photographer
Richard Pountney, retired musician
Henry Tomlinson, retired musician

The official forces

Colonel de Montfort, chief constable of the area
Inspector Forrester, of the local police

and a large supporting cast

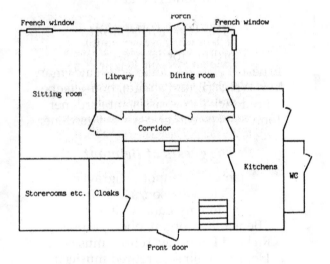

Plan of 'Belmont' (not to scale)

One

A very curious characteristic of my good friend, Mr Sherlock Holmes, was that even on those rare occasions where he erred in his interpretation of one – or more – of the aspects of a case, none the less he usually managed in some singular manner to arrive at a solution of the mystery, while everyone else remained baffled. One instance was that which I shall now describe, a case which I myself was the means of bringing to Holmes's attention.

It was, I recall, a seasonably hot day early in July, 1899. I had slept badly, owing to the oppressive heat, which in London seems confined and intensified, trapped in some manner by the buildings. In the end I gave up the attempt even to rest, and came down to my breakfast early. I had thus finished and had begun to read the newspaper in earnest when Sherlock Holmes entered the room. He nodded to me and seemed about to speak, but then his gaze wandered to the corner of the room. He raised an eyebrow, and sighed.

'It is the future, Holmes!' said I, following his example and staring at the telephone which we had recently had installed, after much persuasion on my part and some reluctance on Holmes's.

'Perhaps it is,' said he, 'but I see many disadvantages to it.'

'It is well tried,' I told him. 'It is now fully twenty years since the first London exchange opened …'

'Remind me to send a congratulatory telegram to the Postmaster General,' said Holmes, rather churlishly.

'To begin with, there were only eight subscribers ...'

'I have some trifling recollection that you have already favoured me with lengthy extracts from the prospectus, Doctor,' said Holmes.

'But think, Holmes! Consider the ease with which one may communicate with one's fellows! Why, it is exactly like having your very own little telegraph office in the house!' said I.

'With its own little bell, constantly interrupting one's meals ...'

At that juncture, the telephone bell rang.

'Constantly interrupting one's meals,' repeated Holmes firmly, picking up the receiver with every expression of distaste. There followed one of those curious one-sided and monosyllabic conversations which have become so very familiar to all of us in recent years. After a moment, Holmes held the instrument out to me. 'So far as I can judge, Doctor, the caller wishes to speak to you,' he said.

'Thank you, Holmes.' I took the telephone cautiously, for – although we had had the instrument in the house for a couple of days now – this was the first person to contact me in this fashion. 'Hello? This is Dr Watson speaking.'

The receiver emitted a strange crackle, over which I could hear occasional stray fragments of speech. '... Watson? ... Morrison here, at Belmont. You had arranged ... stay with us ... some ... ago. I thought ... telephone ... confirm your arrival later today.'

'Yes, yes, indeed,' said I. 'I am packed and ready for the off! All being well, I shall arrive there in the middle of the afternoon. I look forward to my stay.'

'... look forward to ... you. My compliments, sir.'

'And mine to you, sir! There you are, Holmes,' I said, replacing the receiver, 'that was Mr Morrison, the secretary at Belmont. Wanted to confirm my stay there, beginning this afternoon.'

'But I thought you had already confirmed it by letter?' said Holmes, with a smile.

'Well, I had. Even so, there may have been some unexpected difficulty, some reason why I could not go. The telephone avoids having to worry about sending telegrams, or disappointing people at the last minute.'

'Then perhaps I shall grow to like it,' said Holmes calmly. 'In any event, I sincerely trust you will enjoy your holiday.'

'Thank you. Lord knows, I am ready enough for a change,' said I frankly, 'I grow tired of London in this weather, and yearn for some country air.'

'You should get plenty of that,' said Holmes. 'Is this place not set 'twixt the North Downs and the Weald? You will forgive the poetic description, which, if I mistake not, was in that particular prospectus. From which I also heard numerous extracts.'

'It was a trifle overblown,' I agreed. 'But, yes, it is on the borders of Surrey and Sussex, and ... according to the friend who recommended it to me, or, rather, me to it ... it is a delightful spot.'

'The area is indeed delightful,' said Holmes. 'And with some most interesting associations for both of us, for you will recall that intriguing ... though rather elementary ... affair of the Cunninghams, which took place not far from there?'

'I do recall it, Holmes. In fact, I recorded it under the title of "The Reigate Puzzle".'

'I looked into it,' said he. 'And I must confess that I have seldom encountered such an emphasis on sensationalism at the expense of fact. By the by,' he added, before I could fairly counter this charge, 'does Colonel Hayter still live in those parts?'

'He does.' Colonel Hayter was an old friend whom I had first known in Afghanistan, and with whom Holmes and I had been staying at the time of the Cunningham case. 'Colonel Hayter had suggested I stay with him, in point of fact. But I fear he is not the man he once was, and any excitement ... even an unobtrusive guest such as myself ... is quite forbidden. He lives quietly these days, his only companions a nurse, for he is very weak, and a secretary of some sort, a Carstairs, or Carruthers, or some such name. The colonel is working on what he has described to me as his 'literary testament', in the shape of a definitive history of the events at Maiwand. The secretary ... a young fellow, fresh from university, as I understand ... is helping him to compile it, and I have offered to pay a short visit tomorrow, to look over what has been accomplished thus far, and perhaps offer some advice on the literary and military aspects.'

'I see. You will please to give the colonel my compliments and good wishes. I owe him much, for he was the means of introducing me to a most diverting case,' said Holmes, buttering a slice of toast. 'Tell me,' said he, 'you had mentioned earlier that you were introduced to this place, and not it to you. What meant you by that?'

'The place is not an hotel,' I told him. 'It is an old country house ... Belmont by name ... which is run under the terms of a charitable trust.'

'Indeed?'

'The trust was set up some twenty years ago by a philanthropist whose name ... could I but recollect it myself ... would be familiar to you. A household name, in very truth, for he made a vast fortune in boot-blacking or some such thing, invested it in railway stock, and so became one of the richest men in England. Now, he was by way of being a patron of the arts ... indeed, he was himself a talented amateur engraver in mezzotint ...'

Holmes groaned.

I ignored him. 'He had a large family ... and, by what I am told privately, an equally large wife. He realized that many of his artistic acquaintances were in much the same state. He realized further that many of them would benefit from the occasional break from home, wife and children, but that most of them simply had insufficient funds to permit their taking a holiday abroad, or staying at a first-rate hotel. He accordingly bought this old manor house, and endowed it in his will with the wherewithal to run it exactly like one of those first-rate hotels, but at a nominal cost to guests.'

'A philanthropist indeed.'

'As you say, Holmes.'

'And the recommendation?'

'Oh,' said I, 'one needs a recommendation from someone who has stayed there, nothing more than that. Provided that one has some connection with literature, or the arts. Oh, and the terms of the trust mean that only men can stay there, of course.'

'So that there may be no distractions, presumably?' said Holmes.

'Presumably. You ought to come along, Holmes ... I could ring the secretary now, see if they have a room free.'

'You are very kind. But I fear my literary achievements are scarcely an adequate testimonial.'

'You underrate yourself, Holmes. Why, your monographs have invariably been received as the last word on their subject ... whatever it may have been.'

Holmes laughed. 'I am tempted. But it is very short notice. And besides, I can hardly leave just at the moment, when this business of the black pearl of the Borgias is so very pressing.'

I nodded, for I knew that Holmes was engaged on trying to track down the thief who had stolen the fabulous jewel from the Prince of Colonna's room at the Dacre Hotel. I may add that the case baffled even Holmes for a time, although he solved the puzzle a year later in a most interesting case which I have recorded under the title, *The Six Napoleons*.

'Did I overhear you say your bag is packed?' asked Holmes.

'You did. I am all ready, and shall leave by the afternoon train ... unless, of course, I can be of any assistance with your investigations, in which case I am entirely at your disposal.'

Holmes shook his head. 'Thank you for the offer, but I fear that the problem may be insoluble, at least for the moment, and that your best efforts would not help me. I suspect that it will prove to be one of those annoying cases where the solution, if it comes at all, is delayed some considerable time, and is largely dependent on chance. No, Doctor, it only remains for me to wish you an enjoyable and restful holiday in the country. And that I must do now,' he added, looking at his watch, 'for I have an appointment at half past the hour. Princes are not to be kept waiting, even when one brings them no good news.'

Holmes left shortly afterwards, and I spent the morning putting the finishing touches to my packing, although in truth my wants were few and simple.

I took a cab at eleven, lunched at my club, and at two o'clock was sitting in a first-class carriage at Victoria. At Redhill I changed to a local train, and at half past three I got down at a quiet little halt, set amongst poppies and cow parsley. I had been given directions to the house, which was no more than half a mile from the railway halt, and a leisurely walk of ten minutes or so brought me to a leafy lane, with a few large houses strung out along it. Mostly these were newly built, the homes of City men indulging their taste for the country, but one of them was genuinely old, the exterior dating as I judged from the early part of the seventeenth century. A new and brightly polished brass plaque on the gatepost read 'Belmont', and I turned into a gravel drive that led through neat gardens. I nodded a greeting to an old fellow who was pottering about in the flower beds, and stopped before a heavy oak door, over which was carved the date 1607. Pleased that my deduction had been correct, I pulled vigorously at the bell.

There was a short delay, then the door swung open with a creak, to reveal a short man, some forty-odd years old, deeply sunburned, with a very straight back and wearing the broadest grin I have ever seen. 'Yes, sir?'

'My name is Watson,' said I. 'I believe I am expected?'

'Dr Watson? You are indeed, sir. Come in, and I'll bring your bag along.'

'Thank you, Mr …'

'Welsh, sir. Ernest Welsh … Ernie to my pals … gardener and handyman round about the old place. My wife would have met you, but it's almost tea time.'

I went in, and found myself in a spacious entrance hall, panelled in dark oak. On the opposite side, facing the door, a couple of steps led up to a sort of raised dais which formed a corridor running left and right, with a balustrade along its length. On the corridor wall, again right opposite the front door, hung a very large and rather indifferent painting of a dour-looking gentleman dressed in the style of fifty years ago.

'The founder of the place, that, sir,' said Welsh, seeing me looking at the picture. 'Now, as you are just in time for tea, why not go straight through to the library ... that door, there, sir ... and meet the other gentlemen? I'll take your bag up to your room, and the wife will show you where it is when you have had a cup of tea.'

'I'm obliged,' said I, and made to give him a small token of my appreciation.

'Bless you, sir, no need for that. When you leave, of course, if you're of the same mind ...' and he gave a sort of half-salute.

The salute, coupled with his carriage, emboldened me to venture on another deduction. 'Old soldier?' I asked.

'That I am, sir.'

'Me too. Berkshires. Wounded at Maiwand, and left the service.'

'Were you, sir? I was in the Sudan, myself, sir.'

'What, this last business?'

'No, sir, about the time you were fighting ... time of General Gordon.'

'Warm work.'

The grin grew broader. 'It was that, sir. And I was similar to yourself, if I may make so bold, for I too took a bullet and was pensioned off. Still, keep smiling, that's what I always say, sir. I fell into this billet almost at once, and have been here ever since.'

'Better to be born lucky than rich, eh?'

'It is, sir. Now, they say it's a small world, and so it is, for haven't the Berkshires just finished the job we ... General Gordon and myself ... started in the Sudan?'

'They have indeed,' said I.

'Gave 'em what for, didn't they, sir?'

'So the newspaper reports say.'

'Well, sir, it's been grand talking to you, if you'll pardon the liberty. But I must be about my work, or the secretary will be after me. Perhaps I'll have the privilege of a word or two later, sir, if you happen to be about the garden and have a moment to spare?'

'With pleasure,' said I.

13

'Then I hope you enjoy your stay, sir.'

'If the guests are all as agreeable as you, Welsh, I shall enjoy myself very much,' I told him, and the honest fellow flushed with pride.

I went up the shallow stair and a couple of paces brought me to the room which Welsh had indicated. It was empty, and I looked round with some curiosity. The room was evidently used as a library of sorts, for though not very large it was lined with books, many in a lamentable state of preservation. A low table held a tray with cups, saucers and light refreshments.

I hesitated, wondering whether to presume to sit down uninvited. A footstep outside heralded the entry of a woman, forty or so years of age and still very handsome, carrying a tray with two teapots upon it.

She put the tray down, and smiled at me. 'Dr Watson, is it?'

'It is.'

'Mrs Welsh, sir. I'm the housekeeper here.'

'Ah, yes, I believe I met your husband.'

'Help yourself to tea, sir, and cake. Darjeeling in this pot, Earl Grey in the other.'

So saying, Mrs Welsh left. I fear that I still stood looking round the room, for, despite the warm and civil reception from Mr and Mrs Welsh, I had not thus far encountered what I might call an official personage. Before too long, however, the door opened again, and a man of around my own age, with a cheerful look on his face, came in.

'Hullo!' said he. 'Dr Watson, I presume?' (In common with every medical man, I have been obliged to grow accustomed to this sort of greeting, since the famous encounter between Stanley and Livingstone.)

'I am, sir.'

He held out his hand. 'Gordon Morrison, sir. Secretary to the trust. I am glad that you arrived this week, for I am off on a short holiday on Friday, and would have been sorry to have missed you. I rather like to meet new guests, introduce myself, and the house, as it were. Do help yourself to tea.'

I poured a cup for Morrison, another for myself, and said, 'You will forgive my making myself at home, but Mr and Mrs Welsh asked me in.'

'I would not have forgiven you had you stood on ceremony,' he said. 'We try to make our guests feel as if they are in their own family home, but with none of the distractions that the family home too often contains. And ... whilst we do not, of course, encourage any sort of familiarity among the servants ... we do not have too many rules and regulations. You have brought a dress suit?' he added anxiously.

'As you asked, sir.'

'We do keep up certain standards. Although,' he added with a sigh, 'some of the guests ... still, I must not talk out of school.'

'A friend of mine once remarked that art in the blood is liable to take strange forms,' I told him.

'It is indeed! And, after three or four years in this post, I can say that some of the forms it takes are strange in the extreme. I confess that I had not fully realized the meaning of the word "Bohemianism" before I came here.'

'The artistic temperament,' said I.

'Lord, yes! But I fear I run the risk of offending you, Doctor, for you are yourself a man of letters.'

'I flatter myself that I am a practical man, sir, without too many fads and fancies,' I reassured him.

The door opened at this point, and three men entered together, talking in an animated fashion. The conversation tailed off as they saw me, and Morrison made the necessary introductions. 'Gentlemen, this is Dr Watson. Doctor, may I introduce Mr Peter Gregson, sculptor?'

Gregson extended his hand. 'Delighted, Doctor.'

'As am I, sir. I know a Gregson,' said I. 'Policeman ... inspector, in fact, at Scotland Yard.'

'Hardly the most artistic of occupations,' said Gregson with a smile.

'Perhaps not, sir,' I told him, 'but it does ensure that honest citizens ... artists included ... can sleep easy in their beds!'

Gregson considered me closely for a moment. 'A touch, Doctor! A man of principle, evidently ... and not afraid to stick

15

by your principles. I foresee that we shall have some interesting discussions. But I am being rude,' he said to Morrison, 'for I interrupted your introductions, Secretary.'

'Mr James Davenport, engraver,' said Morrison.

'Sounds quite like "Happy Families", does Gordon's introduction!' rumbled Davenport. He was a huge man, and the hand he held out to me resembled nothing so much as a bear's paw.

'We like to know what our fellow guests do for a living,' said Morrison, no whit perturbed. 'Saves any embarrassment, we find.'

'Embarrassment?' said I, puzzled.

'Well,' said Morrison with a laugh, 'some of our guests ... present company honourably excepted, of course ... do have a rather high opinion of themselves and their talents. So, they can be offended if strangers ask "What do you do for a living?" you see. And you're not to mind James, Doctor. He can be somewhat uncultivated at times. And finally, Mr Jeremy Lane. You should get on with the doctor, Lane, for you're both writers.'

We murmured the usual pleasantries, and a general conversation of a desultory sort ensued, during which I was able to study my fellow guests more closely. Gregson was about my own age, dressed in what was almost a foppish adherence to the latest fashion.

Davenport was a few years younger; he had a bushy beard, and was somewhat stout, although he carried it well for he was, as I say, considerably taller than the average; a large man in every sense, I thought, with a great, deep bass voice to match the rest of him.

Lane was only twenty-odd, again fashionably dressed, though not excessively so, and he had an almost permanent cynical smile which I soon found slightly irritating; too much the popular image of the literary man, I felt, although I reminded myself of the inadvisability of making hasty judgements.

When we had finished tea, Morrison rang the bell and asked Mrs Welsh to show me my room. She led the way upstairs, and opened a door. 'Here you are, Doctor. There are no keys, but you'll find a bolt on the inside. Although most of the gentlemen don't bother, for the house has never been troubled by tramps, or anything of that sort.'

'Then I am sure I shall not bother either,' I said.

Mrs Welsh left, and I went inside my room and looked round. It was larger than I had expected, and I decided that the house must have been extended considerably since it was first built, a conclusion I later learned was correct. There was a large table under the window, and I strolled across to it. Several pens – mostly the worse for wear – were set out on the table, together with an ink-well and paper, evidently put there lest literary inspiration should strike unexpectedly.

Moving to the side of the table, I glanced out into the garden at the back of the house. The area immediately round the house was immaculate, although there were traces of neglect at the farther end. Welsh, along with a couple of other men, his assistants or labourers, as I took it, was busy at work, and the whole formed an idyllic picture. I promised myself a delightful fortnight in a spot which seemed every bit as enchanting as the purple prose in the prospectus – which, I had learned at tea, had been written by a guest, himself a minor poet of some renown – had suggested.

I bathed and changed my clothes, and at seven o'clock I was again in the little book-lined room – the 'library', as Welsh had rather grandly styled it – to take a companionable glass of sherry with the other guests. Three other men, whom I had not thus far met, joined us. Morrison introduced me to Mr Henry Tomlinson and Mr Richard Pountney, both elderly gentlemen who were introduced to me as retired musicians. And, just as we were about to go in to dinner, the last guest arrived, a Mr Benjamin Morgan, who showed every sign of having changed hurriedly and bathed not at all.

At dinner it emerged that Morgan was a photographer, and that his late arrival had been occasioned by his having been out on the Downs, taking pictures in the glorious sunlight. And Tomlinson and Pountney explained that I had missed them earlier because they too been out for the afternoon, but only as far as the local inn, for they made no claim to be as energetic as some of the younger men.

There was a curious little incident at dinner, which I was later to remember. I experienced that indefinable sensation of being studied closely, with which most readers will be familiar, though they could not begin to explain it, any more than I can – some almost-forgotten atavistic trait from our primeval days, I suppose. Anyway, I glanced up, and caught Morgan studying me closely. I could think of nothing to say, but was saved the trouble, for Morgan flushed like any schoolgirl, and said, 'Your pardon, sir. I was merely thinking what a fine subject you would make for the camera.'

There was a general laugh at this, and I confess that I was unsure how to take it. However, Morrison reassured me by saying, 'You must not mind Morgan, Doctor. He has said the same to all of us.'

'Except me!' amended Gregson.

'Oh,' said Morgan, 'you're quite vain enough as it is!'

It was not said unkindly; and there was another general laugh; yet for all that, I felt that there was something more unpleasant, some antagonism which was only barely concealed beneath the banter.

The moment passed at once, and there ensued a general conversation, on the hoary old topic, 'Is Photography Art?' I shall not rehearse the entire argument, which will be all too familiar to readers of the popular press; but there was an interesting and – in view of later events, perhaps a significant – divergence of opinion. Morgan naturally took the view that photography was not merely art, but The Art, in capitals, the one, the only, the true. Some of the others took the opposite view, the most articulate being Gregson. 'Why,' said he, 'all a man need do is press a button, and lo! ... a work of art. Your instruction books tell you what to do, how, when and why to do it. Even your ground-glass screen is engraved with lines to show you The Golden Mean! How can you ...' etc., etc.

My own opinion was sought, and I freely confessed that I had no strong feelings either way. This brought me a certain amount of cheerful contumely, as being something of a

Philistine, but at least it concluded the aimless discussion, and the conversation turned to lighter things.

There was a piano in a corner of the spacious dining room, and it turned out that Tomlinson, who had been something of a singer in his day, still had a fine baritone voice. He favoured us with a couple of songs after dinner, and I was looking forward to a diverting enough evening. However, I was to be disappointed, for, to my surprise, most of the guests excused themselves and went up their rooms at which I considered an exceptionally early hour.

Morrison evidently noticed my disappointment, and told me, 'Unless you visit the local inn ... which is not entirely salubrious, I may say ... there is little to do of an evening. For that reason, and because they do come here for a rest, most of our gentlemen do not keep late hours. However, it is a little early for me, too, so perhaps a turn round the garden would not come amiss?'

'Indeed not,' said I. 'And possibly even a cigar?'

'I should be delighted.'

The dining room had an enormous French window, which took up the angle of the outside walls, but the evening had turned slightly chilly, and the windows were shut, so Morrison led me to a small door, which he opened to reveal a tiny porch of sorts.

'This was the old door, here before French windows were thought of,' said he. 'And you will note ...' and he pointed with some pride at the telephone which had pride of place on a wall of the porch. 'The coming thing,' said he.

'Just what I was telling a friend of mine this morning,' I said. 'I can see the day when every household will have one of these.'

'Well, perhaps I would not go quite that far,' said Morrison with a smile. 'But for the man of business, yes, I predict that the telephone will quickly become indispensable.'

He opened the door in the outer wall of the little porch, and ushered me out into the June evening.

'Welsh and his fellows certainly do a good job with your gardens,' I told him.

19

'They do what they can, although the place is a little too large for the staff I have,' he said. 'The old difficulty ... the trust income, once more than adequate, is no longer as impressive as it was. I should like to have the money to improve the entire garden, some day. There are all sorts of nooks and crannies ... there is even an old walled fruit garden, dating from the last century, which you will see if you take a look round in daylight tomorrow. Overgrown now, of course, but with great capabilities, as a more famous gardener than I am was wont to remark. Gardening is by way of being a hobby of mine,' he went on. 'Before I came down here, I worked in a City firm, but I find the country far more congenial. As indeed is the position ... you will have noticed that many of us are on first-name terms, the result of acquaintance over the years. This job is, to be blunt, something of a sinecure, for the place pretty well runs itself, and my attendance is required only on Mondays and Fridays, as a rule.'

'You do not live in the house itself, then?' I asked.

'I have a cottage of sorts a couple of miles down the lane,' said Morrison. 'Only small, but with a large garden. I should have been off home some time ago, in the usual way of things, but I am staying here overnight ... I have a camp bed in my room upstairs ... and putting in an extra day tomorrow. I believe I mentioned that I am off on holiday at the weekend? I wanted to clear up as much as may be before I left.'

We finished our cigars, and said good night. Perhaps it was the country air, or perhaps I was fatigued by the day's travel and the meeting of new people. Whatever the cause, and despite the hour's still being somewhat earlier than my habitual bedtime, I knew nothing more until eight o'clock next morning, when a tap on the door heralded my early morning tea.

I had made an appointment to see Colonel Hayter that day, and so I decided to leave a fuller exploration of the grounds for later in the week. I was familiar enough with the area as a whole, although not with the immediate environs of Belmont, and saw from a glance at a framed map in the library that a walk of some three or four miles would bring me to Colonel Hayter's house at Reigate.

I set off after breakfast, taking the path that led through the garden at the back of the house. I noticed the walled garden Morrison had mentioned, although I had no time to go in and look round. As I passed the old brick wall, I saw Gregson, standing in front of an easel, and looking somewhat disgruntled.

'I thought you were a sculptor?' said I, after exchanging the usual civilities.

'I am, but I paint as well. That reminds me, you have not seen a palette knife about the place at all, have you? I've mislaid mine, and I foolishly only brought the one along.'

'You mean those little trowel sort of things? Afraid not. Do you not have some brushes there?'

'I do,' said Gregson. 'But I prefer the direct approach of the knife.'

'Indeed? I have known surgeons who thought much the same.'

He regarded me suspiciously. I added hastily, 'No, I fear I have not seen one about the place. But I'll keep an eye open for it.'

'I should be most grateful if you would.'

I set off in earnest then along the foot of the Downs, and quickly came to a landmark I recognized. On old ground now, I made good time and arrived at the colonel's house towards eleven. I found my old friend harshly treated by the hand of Time, so weak indeed that he could scarcely rise to greet me.

There was a second guest at lunch, another military man, Colonel de Montfort, who turned out to be the chief constable of those parts. And there was, naturally enough, a good deal of reminiscence on a wide spectrum of matters: criminal, military and sporting. Colonel Hayter seemed to enjoy himself well enough, but the excitement, or the effort, of so many recollections of stirring deeds tired him out very quickly, so that by the middle of the afternoon both the nurse and the secretary – whose name was Cameron, by the way, not that he will appear again in my tale – indicated that it might be as well if de Montfort and I said our goodbyes.

'I'm going your way, Doctor,' said de Montfort as we emerged into the sunshine. 'May I offer you a lift?'

I was somewhat weary from my morning's exercise and somewhat disturbed at finding my old friend in so sad a state, so I did not stand out but accepted the colonel's kind offer.

On the drive back, we chatted of this and that, until the trap turned into the lane which led to Belmont. The colonel's driver, who had not thus far ventured upon any familiarity, coughed and said, 'Beg pardon, sir, but there looks to be something to do at the gentleman's house here.'

'What? Lord, yes, you're right, Williams,' said the colonel. 'A bad business, too, by the look of things,' he added, gesturing to a low, covered vehicle that stood in the lane, 'for that is our mortuary cart. There may be a call for your services, Doctor, so perhaps ...'

'I am entirely at your disposal, sir,' said I.

'Then you stay here, Williams, while we take a look at this business.' And so saying, the colonel jumped down and led the way to the gate, where a young constable stood on duty.

'Now, what ...' and the colonel broke off as another man emerged from the house. 'Ah ... Forrester!'

The man so addressed ran down the drive. 'My word, Colonel, you have soon heard of the matter!' said he. 'And Dr Watson, too!'

Before he had spoken, I had recognized him, for this was another old acquaintance, Inspector Forrester, who had been involved in the Cunningham case a decade earlier. We shook hands, and Forrester said, 'Is Mr Sherlock Holmes with you, by any chance, Doctor?'

'He is not,' I said.

Forrester's face fell. 'I could wish he were, sir,' said he, 'for I tell you frankly that this is a bad business.'

'We know nothing of it,' said de Montfort. 'I am here purely by chance. So perhaps you had better explain?'

'I must ask you, Doctor, what you know of a Mr Benjamin Morgan?' said Forrester.

'I? Nothing. I met Morgan for the first time in my life last night,' I told him.

22

'So, he was not a particular friend of yours?'

'No, although he seems likeable enough. Say, though ... you said "was", did you not?'

'I did, sir. I regret to inform you that Mr Benjamin Morgan has been murdered.'

Two

'**M**urdered?' I asked rather stupidly – for even my long association with Holmes had scarcely prepared me for this tragedy, so very unexpected, and so very close to home.

'Stabbed, I'm afraid,' said Forrester. 'In that little porch affair, where the telephone is.'

Feeling somewhat foolish, I asked, 'He was not by any chance killed with an artist's palette knife, was he?'

'That's an odd sort of question, Doctor,' said Forrester.

De Montfort added, 'An odd sort of weapon, too, if you ask me. The artist's palette knives I've seen have had a rounded end, rather after the manner of a cheese knife. No damn good for stabbing! Unless you mean the other sort, like a little … what d'you call 'em? … a bricklayer's trowel kind of contraption. Still a bit small, and rough and ready, but you might do some damage with one of those, if you had a determined man with a strong arm behind it.'

'Why did you ask that particularly, Doctor?' Forrester wanted to know.

My feelings of foolishness in no degree abated, I said, 'Oh … it was nothing. Nothing really. Just something that happened this morning. Rather silly … an odd incident, the kind that lodges in your mind. One of the guests happened to ask me if I had seen his palette knife around the place, as he had mislaid it.'

'And which of the gentlemen might that have been?' asked Forrester.

'Chap called Gregson,' I told him.

'I see.' Forrester raised an eyebrow.

'Well, Inspector?' asked de Montfort, with some warmth.

'No, gentlemen,' said Forrester, 'Mr Morgan was not killed with a palette knife, but with a paper knife. A letter opener, some people call them. Silver, rather ornate.'

'Indeed?' said de Montfort.

In an absent sort of way, Forrester said, 'The paper knife ... like the missing palette knife ... belonged to Mr Gregson.'

'Indeed!' said de Montfort again.

'He claims it was upstairs in his room.'

'And who found the body?' I asked.

'That was Mr Gregson again.'

De Montfort and I looked at one another. 'I think you had better give us a sketch of events as far as you know them,' said de Montfort.

'It was this way, sir,' said the inspector. 'It appears that this Mr Gregson wished to make a telephone call. He went into the cubbyhole where the telephone is, tried the number, but failed to make his call. He set off for the front door to smoke a cigarette, and as he left the dining room, Mr Morgan went in, also intending to use the telephone. Mr Gregson had his smoke, and went back to try again. The dining room was empty, and the inner door to the porch was closed. Mr Gregson approached the door, but could not hear anything. Thinking that Mr Morgan must have finished and left, Mr Gregson opened the door ... and Mr Morgan's body fell out, literally at Mr Gregson's feet.'

'Good Lord!' I said. 'That must have been a considerable shock for the poor fellow!'

'To say the least,' said the inspector. 'According to the gardener chap, Mr Gregson started screaming "blue murder", and "fit to wake the dead".'

'An unfortunate choice of phrases in the circumstances,' said de Montfort, drily.

'Indeed, sir. And Mr Gregson is still very upset.' Forrester hesitated.

De Montfort said, 'You seem to imply a "But ..."'

There was another hesitation, then Forrester said, 'But ... and despite his distress, which seems genuine enough ... things look very bad for Mr Gregson, and that's the truth. It was his knife, which he says he last saw upstairs in his room, which was used to kill Mr Morgan. It was Mr Gregson who was outside the dining room ... if indeed he was outside ... when Mr Morgan was in there. Nobody else seems to have been downstairs, or at any rate not near the dining room.'

'But they would scarcely advertise the fact if they were!' I told him. I marched up to the front door, which I have already described as heavy oak, set in the ancient thick stone wall. 'The wall is thick, as you see, forming an entrance lobby of sorts here,' I went on. 'If Gregson merely stood in the open doorway, looking out at the garden, he would be unlikely to see anyone creeping along to the dining room door. If he actually came outside into the garden, then it would be well-nigh impossible for him to see anyone in the house.'

'He says he came just outside the door,' said Forrester.

'So that someone might have sneaked along to the dining room,' I said.

Forrester looked unconvinced.

'Well, then,' said I, striving to emulate Holmes's methods as much as may be, 'let us consider the alternative. Was the outer door to the porch closed?'

'Closed, but not locked. In fact, Mr Gregson had originally gone into the porch from the garden, using the outer door.'

'There you are!' I said in some triumph. 'The murderer might easily have entered from the garden!'

Forrester shook his head. 'I hardly think so, Doctor. The door was unlocked, fair enough, but the gardener, Welsh, and his lad, Merryweather, were out there pretty well all the time. Now, I don't claim that one or the other of them was never out of sight of the house, or that one or the other never came inside. In fact, we know that Welsh came in for a cup of tea at around the time in question ... which was three o'clock this afternoon, by the by, almost to the minute, so far as we can judge. But the lad did not; he took his tea outside. So, for all practical purposes, one or another of those two was outside the whole time, and they never saw anyone come near the outer door.'

'Done from the inside, then,' said de Montfort.

'It seems almost certain, sir.' Forrester hesitated again. 'You'll recall I asked if Mr Holmes was with you, Doctor? Well, the colonel here knows me, and my abilities, well enough not to take me amiss when I say honestly that I wish Mr Holmes were here, for I'm pretty well out of my depth, and that's a fact. In the decade since we last met, I've had seven cases of sudden death to deal with. Two were suicides, poor souls; three were accidents; one was the result of a drunken brawl; and the last one was a henpecked husband who killed his nagging wife, then went along to the local station and turned himself in to the sergeant, nice as ninepence! So, you'll understand that my experience of these affairs is limited.'

'Well spoken, Inspector,' said de Montfort. 'And you'll know me well enough not to take me amiss when I echo your wish that Mr Holmes should look into this business. How about it, Doctor? Could you not persuade him to investigate on our behalf? As Forrester, says, we are a collection of mossbacks here, and need some help.'

'I can ask him,' I said. 'But I happen to know that he is very busy just now, and I can promise nothing.'

De Montfort looked crestfallen. 'I am sorry to hear you say so. Well, I suppose I shall just have to appeal to Scotland Yard, ask them to send out Inspector Lestrade, or another of their best men.'

'Good Heavens, no!' said I, adding hastily, 'That is to say, I am sure that I can prevail on Holmes to take a look at the matter.'

De Montfort held out a hand. 'I shall be eternally grateful! And now, Inspector, unless I can be of any further use, I must be going along. You will please be good enough to keep me informed?' And he made his farewells and was soon in his trap going back the way we had come.

'Well, Forrester,' said I, when the colonel was out of sight, 'you are quite sure that having Holmes here will not ...'

'Not in the least, sir. I spoke the literal truth when I told you that this is out of my depth. I have not the driving ambition of some of my fellows ... I'd far rather have my garden and my pipe than be chasing all over London. Oh, I'm well enough for the usual run of crime round here, but this ... no, sir, if Mr Holmes will consent to look at the problem, I'd be very grateful.'

'I could call him now, for we have the telephone at Baker Street,' I said. 'That is, if it is quite in order to use the telephone, or ...'

'We have examined the porch very thoroughly,' said Forrester, 'but there was nothing to be made of that, apart from a few bloodstains on the floor, as you would expect.'

'The murderer's clothing might well have been bloodstained, too,' I pointed out.

'I had thought of that, sir. And we did indeed find some bloodstains.'

'Oh?'

'Yes ... on Mr Gregson's trousers.'

'Understandable, if the body had fallen against him?'

'True, Doctor, but another fact which some might regard as telling against him, if not positively damning.'

'Well,' said I, 'that's as may be. I'll ring Holmes now, see what he thinks of it all.' And I went into the house, up the shallow stair and into the large dining room. The door to the little porch stood open, and so did the outer door. The bloodstains of which Forrester had spoken had evidently been washed away, and the bright June sunlight streamed in; but even that could not prevent a shudder of horror coming involuntarily over me as I picked up the telephone and asked the exchange to connect me with 221B.

The bell pealed for what seemed an eternity, and I was just thinking that Holmes must still be out on business, when a youthful but hoarse voice said, ''Ullo? Oo's there?'

Recognizing the page's voice and style of oratory, I said, 'Billy? Is that you? This is Dr Watson ... is Mr Holmes there?'

'Mr 'Olmes, Doctor? No, 'e's out.'

'Now, Billy, listen to me ... I want you to ask Mr Holmes to ring me as soon as he gets back. The number is on a piece of paper on the mantelshelf. Have you got that?'

'Yes, sir. Mr 'Olmes to ring you, on the mantelshelf. Right you are, Doctor.'

Knowing that I could easily try again later should Holmes not be equal to the task of breaking Billy's cryptogram, I replaced the receiver, and rejoined Forrester in the dining room.

'Now, Doctor,' said the inspector, 'although Mr Holmes is not here, you are, and you can be of some valuable service to me.'

'I am entirely at your disposal.'

'The first thing is, would you view Mr Morgan's body? It was taken into the library next door. The police surgeon has seen it already, of course, and I don't for one moment imagine that your opinion will differ from his, but Mr Holmes is sure to ask about the wound, and so on, and if you've seen it at first hand, so to speak ...'

'I quite understand.'

Forrester took me to the library, where the body of the unfortunate Morgan lay. I examined it thoroughly, but could find nothing that the police surgeon might have missed. The cause of death was quite obvious, a single stab wound to the heart. The knife which had been found in the body was there, and I made to pick it up gingerly.

'It has been examined for finger marks,' said Forrester. 'We are not so backward, even here.'

'And the results?'

'Nothing very conclusive. Some smudges which "might be anything", according to my man, and one clear print, of Mr Gregson's right index finger.'

'As one might expect, since it was his knife.'

'True enough,' agreed Forrester.

'Stabbed from in front, you see?'

'Yes. He must have seen his killer, almost certainly knew him ... as we have already thought. So, he wouldn't have any reason to suspect anything untoward, until ...' Forrester shivered. 'Makes you think, Doctor.'

'It does indeed.'

'What think you to the slight bruising on the forehead?'

'Oh, undoubtedly made post-mortem. Probably when the body fell out of the lobby on to the floor, or perhaps the head hit the wall of the cubicle as he fell over, soon after he died.'

'So the police surgeon thinks. Well, there's nothing much to be made of that, then, but thank you anyway, Dr Watson.'

Forrester led me back to the dining room, and studied the little cubicle which was the location of the crime. 'A bad business.' He shook himself, as if to clear his head of any morbid fancies. 'Now, Doctor, to work! You arrived ... when?'

'Just yesterday afternoon, I fear. So, I have scarcely had the opportunity to form any but the slightest impression of the house or its occupants.'

'So that you had not, for example, seen the letter opener which killed Mr Morgan?'

'I had not.'

'You had not been into Mr Gregson's room, say?'

'Certainly not!'

'Oh, I imply nothing untoward, sir. I just thought he might have invited you in to smoke a cigar, say. Something of that sort.'

'I hardly knew any of them well enough for that sort of thing.'

'Quite so,' said Forrester. 'Now, I understand that it was the custom of the house that guests did not lock their doors?'

'So I was told. I was assured that there had never been any alarms or excursions, no trouble with burglars or anything. With the benefit of hindsight, of course, those assurances ring a little hollow. But then one does not come away for a fortnight's rest with the idea that one will be stabbed to death.'

'Indeed not. Anyway,' said Forrester with a grim smile, 'I suspect that a few of the doors will be locked tonight!'

'I know mine will!' said I frankly. 'For the significance of the testimony of Welsh and his fellows has not escaped me, just as I'm sure it has not escaped you.'

'It has not, Doctor.' Forrester hesitated. 'I know how difficult my next question will be, sir. I know you dislike telling tales out of school, as it were, and in the ordinary way of things, I should not dream of listening to gossip about the gentlemen staying here, much less would I ask you to talk about them. But this is a very grim affair, and with some serious implications which you have already noticed yourself. So, I must ask if you noticed any sort of animosity, any antagonism, between any of the guests? Anything at all, but more especially if Mr Morgan or Mr Gregson were involved?'

I hesitated in my turn, uncertain as to the best course of action. Forrester was right, of course, it was my duty to say plainly as much as I knew. And yet it seemed to smack of disloyalty, even if it were disloyalty to a man I had only just met.

'Come, Doctor, I can see that there is something.'

'Well, then ... and this is purely my own impression, you are to be clear on that score ... but there was a rather unpleasant little interlude at dinner yesterday.' And I proceeded to tell him what had happened.

When I had done, Forrester asked, 'What was your impression of how matters stood between Morgan and Gregson? Was it merely a sort of schoolboy banter, or more earnest, think you?'

'It was handled lightly enough,' said I. 'But for all that, I had the feeling of something more weighty at the back of it, some old antipathy, if not downright hostility.'

'Thank you for your candour, sir,' said Forrester. 'And my apologies again for pressing the matter.'

'Oh, it is hardly your fault, Inspector. Had Morgan not been killed, the situation would never have arisen. Is your work here all but done?'

'I think so, sir. We shall take the body to the mortuary for examination, although I hardly think there will be any surprises there. For the rest, in the absence of any sort of conclusive proof as to motive and so on, I think I shall wait until Mr Holmes arrives. Now, I think I had best see Mr Morrison, and tell him how things stand.'

Forrester left, and I took another look round the room, but without forming any real opinion as to what might have occurred. At the very least, I thought, I might get the geography of the place, as it were, firmly fixed in my mind. When you entered the front door of the house, you were at once in a large hall, too grand to be called a mere lobby, with a stand for umbrellas, pegs for coats and hats, stags' heads, and the like. To the left – as you stood when you first came into the house – was a cloakroom of sorts, with a wash basin and the usual offices. To your right was the main stair, broad and grand, with a massive oak banister that would have been a splendid ornament to any house, and beyond that again was a baize door leading to the kitchens, and the living quarters of Mr and Mrs Welsh. These were out of bounds to guests, save by special invitation.

Directly opposite the main door was another stair of sorts, a shallow flight of three steps only, leading to the long oak-panelled corridor that ran to left and right. In lieu of a wall, an oak railing or baluster ran along the near-side portion of the corridor which abutted on the entrance hall, giving the effect of a raised dais – indeed, I am half convinced that the foundation of the house was much older than the date over the front door might suggest; that this entrance hall was the original part of the house; and that the corridor now ran where once some old lord of the manor had kept his high table.

At the far end of the corridor to the left was a spacious sitting room, all odd angles and nooks, comfortably fitted up like the smoking room of a London club, even down to the billiard table which stood in one corner. This sitting room had French windows which gave on to a little paved area, at the far side of which was a pond, and beyond that was the garden proper.

The little library was to the right of the sitting room, and then the dining room – where I now stood – was on the other side of the library. These three rooms were reached from the corridor, and only from the corridor, there were no connecting doors between them. However, in the right-hand wall of the dining room – looking at it from the door which gave on to the corridor – there was a connecting door leading to the kitchen, and this door was used by Mrs Welsh for serving meals. In the corner made by that same wall, and the wall opposite the corridor, was the huge French window which gave on to the garden. And also in the wall opposite the corridor was the old porch with the telephone.

To complete the plan, at the far right-hand end of the corridor which rang along the house there was another baize door, again leading to the kitchens and staff quarters. (I append a rough sketch of the place which I made at the time, and which may perhaps serve better than a long description.)

Satisfied that I had it pretty clear in my mind, I started towards the porch, thinking I might check the exterior plan. I was interrupted by the opening of the main door, and Forrester saying, 'I'm off now, Doctor. But I shall look in tomorrow, and hope to see yourself and Mr Holmes then.'

He left, and Morrison, looking very gloomy, came into the room. 'A bad business, this, Dr Watson.'

'At least there seems a general consensus as to that point,' I told him.

'What? Oh, indeed.' Morrison looked at me with what seemed like awe. 'I must confess that I had not quite associated you with the Dr Watson of the *Strand*, and such-like, sir. Not until Inspector Forrester mentioned it just now. I understand that you intend to ask Mr Sherlock Holmes to look into the matter?' he added, with a certain access of cheerfulness.

'Indeed, yes. The inspector asked me to do so.'

'I am sure he is right to ask,' said Morrison. 'I can tell you frankly, sir, that I could wish for a speedy ... and, above all, a discreet ... resolution of the matter. As it is, the trustees are hardly likely to look favourably upon my stewardship. After all, I was in the house when it happened!'

'They can scarcely blame you, sir! Unless, of course ...'

'Sir! No, I take your point. But I know my trustees, sir, and you do not. Decent fellows all, of course. But earnest and sober, almost to a fault. Solicitors and clergymen, to a man. Not that I have anything against ... but still! Why, when I think of the publicity ...' and the poor fellow broke off and shook his head in despair.

'I should have no fear on that score,' I told him. 'Inspector Forrester is a good fellow, and I have some small acquaintance with the chief constable. I imagine that they will both want to keep things quiet for the time being. As for Mr Holmes, I can assure you that he is the very soul of discretion. If the matter can be brought to a speedy resolution, there may well be nothing more than a bare summary in the press.'

Morrison looked somewhat relieved, and said, 'Unless you yourself publish some account of it?'

'If ever I do,' I told him, 'you may be certain that I shall hide real names and places in an impenetrable fashion.' (It should perhaps not be necessary for me to add that I have done so in this present account!)

'I am glad to hear you say so,' said Morrison. 'And now, although it seems a touch callous to speak of these things with poor Benjamin lying in the mortuary, the ordinary business of life must needs be attended to. I hardly thought it proper to have dinner in here tonight, and indeed Mrs Welsh has not had time to prepare anything of the usual kind. But I have asked her to put together a cold collation of sorts, and serve it in the sitting room. I have asked that the others assemble in there, so perhaps we should join them?' As he led the way to the door, he added, 'By the way, Doctor, as Mr Holmes is to handle the case, and as you are his friend and colleague, I wonder if you might … discreetly, of course … take the opportunity to ask a few questions, determine where everyone was, and so forth? That is, if you think it a wise idea?'

'Eminently sensible,' said I. 'In fact, I had thought along those lines myself.' This was true enough: I had worked with Holmes long enough to know the value of first-hand evidence taken before Father Time and the fallibility of human memory have conspired to have their usual effect. And if there was a spark of an idea at the back of my mind that I might solve the case before ever Holmes arrived, the reader will understand that such a notion was not unreasonable; these days many of us see ourselves as amateur detectives, and my association with Holmes had at least given me a rudimentary idea of the correct techniques. I followed Morrison to the sitting room, therefore, with some pride and a sturdy determination to do what I might.

Tomlinson and Pountney were already in the sitting room, sunk alike in gloom and leather armchairs. They looked up and nodded as Morrison and I went in, but said nothing.

We sat down. Morrison said, 'In a sense, I'm pleased that I was here; it meant that the police did not have to come and winkle me out from my little cottage, for I should not have wanted my wife upset … not that she won't be, of course, but at least she will hear it from me, not some policeman. On the other hand, it does mean that I am a suspect, just like these old rogues here,' and he nodded towards the other two.

Pountney lifted his head, and smiled wanly without speaking, but Tomlinson stirred in his chair, and said, 'I should have thought there was only one real suspect, wouldn't you?'

'Come, sir,' said Morrison, 'there is hardly a shred of evidence against him that is not purely circumstantial.'

'It was his letter opener, was it not? A letter opener which was in his room? And we all know they did not exactly hit it off. Now, had it been Gregson who was killed, the police would have had excellent reason to suspect any … or all … of us.'

There was an embarrassed silence at this. I felt that I was letting Holmes down, that I should have pressed for further details, but I did not know how to phrase the questions which came unbidden to my mind.

Pountney, evidently anxious to change the subject, asked Morrison, 'How will this affect your holiday, Secretary?'

'Oh, that's scratched, as the turf accountants put it. The police obviously asked me to stay in the district, but even if they hadn't, I wouldn't have felt happy with this looming over me. It would smack of deserting one's post, would it not? No, once this is resolved …'

He broke off as the door swung open and James Davenport came into the room. Davenport nodded, then, evidently feeling that some more elaborate greeting was called for, said, 'This is a damnable affair, is it not?' before walking to the French window that occupied the whole of one wall, where he stood gazing moodily out at the garden.

Davenport's actions seemed to cast an even deeper gloom over the other three occupants of the room, and none of them made any attempt at conversation for a good five minutes. It seemed, to me at least, more like five hours, and I was steeling myself to make some remark about the weather when, to my great relief, the door opened and Jeremy Lane entered the room, brushing back his long blond hair. Lane carried a leatherbound notebook and a silver pencil, and was particularly remarkable inasmuch as he did not seem infected by the prevailing gloom.

He glanced round the room, and cheerfully remarked, 'Very traditional, this.'

'What is, sir?' demanded Davenport in an aggressive fashion.

'Well, all the suspects gathered together, waiting for the detective to tell them who done it. It would have been better in the library, though. Quite the one-act play.'

Davenport said, 'I, for one, don't find that remark funny in the least, you damned puppy! In fact, I think it's offensive in the extreme, and if you haven't got anything sensible to say, I strongly urge you to keep quiet.'

'Sorry, I'm sure! I was just trying to put a brave face on things,' and Lane sat down, temporarily abashed.

'Mrs Welsh is fixing us some sandwiches and things,' said Morrison hastily. The others murmured their thanks, then, not knowing what to say, relapsed into a further silence.

It did not last too long, though, for after a short time the door opened, and Mrs Welsh came in pushing a trolley.

'Good evening, gentlemen.' Mrs Welsh clearly did not see why she should vary her evening greeting just because the house was full of police. After all, her demeanour said as loud as words, she was in the habit of saying the same thing at the start of every dinner, even though she had seen all the guests many times throughout the course of the day. It was one of the little civilities which, to Mrs Welsh, made all the difference.

In exactly the same tone in which she would have apologized for the fact that there was no toast, she went on, 'Sorry about all the upset, but there's nothing we can do about it, is there? Now, the police tell me they have finished in the dining room, so it will be breakfast as usual in there tomorrow. Is that all right? Good, enjoy your meal.'

She gave us a dazzling smile, and headed for the door, stopping to allow Peter Gregson to enter. 'Evening, Mr Gregson, you're just in time for what is, I'm afraid, a very scratch meal.'

Gregson gave her a forced smile, and then came into the room, looked round, and said, 'All been helping the police with their enquiries, have we? Not that any of you have got anything to worry about.'

'I sincerely hope none of us has,' said Morrison, offering Gregson a plate of sandwiches.

'Ugh, no, thanks! I couldn't face anything at the moment. I've never felt less like food in all my life, but I could do with a cup of tea.' Gregson poured himself a cup, added several spoonfuls of sugar, and drank eagerly. He poured a second cup, and placed it on the floor by the side of his chair. He ran a hand through his hair, a habit of his that I had already observed several times yesterday. His hair was longer than convention would have deemed necessary, though not quite as long as Lane's, and despite the fact that he must have been around my own age, it was still a rich tint. His face was unlined, but showing signs of the strain he evidently felt.

He picked his tea up, and drank, in a more leisurely way this time, then, suddenly, he said, 'They think it was me, you know.'

There was a moment's silence at this, then Morrison said, 'I'm sure you're mistaken there. This has obviously been very disturbing for everyone, and equally obviously, all of us here are under some suspicion to some degree or another.'

Gregson shook his head vigorously. 'No, they do. What else could they think, given the circumstances? Perfectly natural, of course. And I know all of you must think the same.'

'Now, there I know you're mistaken,' said Morrison, with a sort of false heartiness that sounded appalling. 'I ...' and even he was unable to continue. He fell silent, and gazed at his plate.

The silence was by turns embarrassing, oppressive and well-nigh intolerable. I was about to say something – anything – to try to clear the air, when all of a sudden Tomlinson put down his plate, stood up and said, 'I know it's a bit early, even for me, but I feel absolutely exhausted. Nervous fatigue, or something of that sort, I expect. So, if you'll all excuse me, I'll say good night.'

'And me,' said Pountney, getting up as well.

As they headed towards the door, Morrison said, 'One moment.' To the room at large, he went on, 'Dr Watson has been good enough to offer to ask Mr Sherlock Holmes to look into this dreadful affair, and should he agree to do so ... and I sincerely hope that he will ... then I would ask you all to answer whatever questions he may put to you. It is, when all is said and done, in our best interests to have it cleared up as quickly as possible. And another thing, which the police probably mentioned to each of you ... and I don't know how much importance you might want to attach to it anyway ... but it might be as well to keep your room door locked, just until all this business can be cleared up. Personally, I take it seriously enough to say that I'm not going to leave my room at all until daylight.'

Gregson stood up, a curious expression on his face. 'There's no need for any of you to worry,' he said. 'I only had the one letter opener with me, and the police have taken that away with them. Of course, there's still the palette knife, isn't there, the one I only pretended to have lost? And then, of course, for all you know, I brought another half-dozen along with me, one for each of you.'

Morrison started to say something, but Gregson went on, almost in a shout, 'I didn't kill Ben! I know you all think I did ... and I can't say that I blame you for that ... but I didn't. Really and truly I didn't!' And he went to the door nearly at a run, brushed past Pountney and Tomlinson, who were standing in the doorway, and hurried out into the corridor.

Pountney stared after him for a long time, then said, 'Well.'

'Well, indeed,' said Tomlinson. 'It seems very much of an anti-climax to say good night after that, but nevertheless, good night.'

Morrison waved a hand as they left, then settled in his chair and looked round at the others. 'I suspect we're all a bit overwrought,' he said. He gazed sternly at Davenport. 'For instance, James, I don't think I've ever heard you swear before today. Certainly not to any great extent.'

Davenport looked suitably ashamed of himself. 'Sorry, Secretary. As you say, our nerves are all a bit frayed just at the moment. I know I'm a bit upset ... a good deal upset ... at all this. You know how it is,' he appealed to his listeners in general ...'a man weighs fifteen stone, or a bit more, has a beard, and a successful enough career, so everyone takes him for some sort of refuge in any of life's little storms. Trustworthy, reliable, and all the rest. To be quite honest, I've never in my whole life come across anything that I could not cope with. Until now, that is. The first ... well, upsetting is the only word that comes to mind, though that is to put it mildly ... the first occurrence in my life that has me at a considerable loss, and so all I can think of to do is show my annoyance by swearing, childish though it may be. I think the real truth of the matter is that I'm very annoyed with myself for feeling so useless. Helpless, almost.' He brooded in silence for a time, then said, 'Poor devil!'

Morrison said, 'You, or Benjamin?'

'Peter Gregson,' said Davenport unexpectedly. 'It does look pretty bad for him, I must say. He was quite right, of course, the police must suspect him, they can't very well do otherwise. And, despite your valiant attempt to reassure him, Gordon, I don't imagine that anyone here has any real doubts.'

'So, you weren't impressed by his rather dramatic ... if not melodramatic ... protestation of innocence?' asked Lane.

Davenport shrugged, but did not reply.

Morrison stood up. 'It does seem to have been a very long day,' he said, 'so I think I'll take a quick look round, make sure everything's locked up, then turn in. Though I imagine Welsh will have been extra vigilant this evening.'

'A bit like bolting the stable door after all the horses have ... well,' said Davenport. 'You know what I mean.'

'Yes. It couldn't really be too much worse if we did leave the front door wide open all night,' said Morrison. 'Still, we might as well at least show willing.'

Davenport stood up. 'I'll make the rounds with you,' he told Morrison. 'We should all feel better after a decent night's sleep.'

As Morrison and Davenport left, Lane looked across at me and said, 'And then there were two. Should we go upstairs together, for safety, do you think, or would you feel happier knowing I wasn't lurking on the staircase behind you?'

There was an odd note in his voice. I could identify the humorous content – or what obviously struck Lane as being humorous – but there was something more, and it took a while to work out what it was. Then I said, 'You're actually quite enjoying this, aren't you?'

Lane had enough grace to look embarrassed. 'Well, you have to admit ... I mean, I feel sorry for the poor chap and all that, but I didn't really know him ... I've only been here a week and it's my first visit ... but you have to admit it's ... well, an opportunity. Isn't it?'

I did not immediately take Lane's meaning. Then I realized the true significance of the leather-bound notebook, open on Lane's knee, and asked, 'You're going to write about this?'

'I really don't see why not,' said Lane, with a defensive shrug of his shoulders. 'After all, everyone says you have to write about what you know, write from your own personal experience. Don't they? And how many writers of sensational fiction have been in this sort of position?'

'This sort of happy position, you mean?'

'You know very well what I mean. I didn't kill Ben Morgan. I am not responsible for his death. But if I can't make a halfway decent book out of the experience, then I really have chosen the wrong career. It may not be well written, but at least it'll be authentic. After all, Doctor, you yourself have done much the same thing on many occasions. The difference between us is that you have a great literary reputation, whereas mine is best described by the good old Latin tag, "non est".'

'Well,' said I with a laugh, 'I suppose that is true enough. Do write your story, and perhaps one day I shall write mine.'

Lane seemed about to speak, when Mrs Welsh came back into the room. 'Dr Watson, someone is asking for you on the telephone, sir.'

'Thank you, Mrs Welsh.'

I went along to the dining room, and into the porch. The outer door was shut and locked, and despite the early hour and the fact that the dining room was bathed in a golden glow of evening sunshine, there was a gloom about the little cubbyhole that might have unsettled a more sensitive soul.

I picked up the receiver, and was heartened to hear Holmes's down-to-earth voice. In a very few words, I explained how matters stood, and asked if he could possibly spare some time.

'I can, and I will, Doctor,' said Holmes, 'for I have run myself into something of a dead end with the Borgia pearl business. I shall take the first convenient train tomorrow.'

'I am delighted to hear it!' said I, and meant it.

I had no key to the outside doors, or I would have taken a stroll in the garden to clear my head, which was swimming from the afternoon's excitement. I could think of nothing to do which might usefully pass the time, so I went into the library and found a book whose solidity promised some narcotic effect. I set off for the stairs, and my eye lit on the umbrella stand, which contained various sticks and the like. One of these was a great ash plant with a massive knotty root for a handle. I had – naturally enough – not brought my revolver with me, not expecting stirring events, so I took the stick upstairs with me. Let anyone try anything untoward with me tonight! I bolted my door, and read until midnight, when my eyes began to close.

The following morning, I went down to breakfast rather late, but found that the others had not yet appeared. I passed the morning somehow or other, I could not say how, although I do know that I was distracted and could not settle down to anything. I was therefore considerably heartened when, towards eleven o'clock, a trap from the local inn pulled up in the lane, and Mr Sherlock Holmes got down from it.

Three

'I have remarked before, Doctor,' said Sherlock Holmes as he strode towards me, 'that you are the stormy petrel of crime, and here you prove me right once again! Apparently in search of peace and quiet, the very first thing you do is encounter a murder!'

'Hardly from choice, Holmes!' I said – and with some indignation, for Holmes's sense of humour is occasionally of the oddest.

'Of course not, Watson. Now, to work. The first thing is to meet the secretary ... Morrison, is it? It is as well to establish our official standing at the outset.'

I knew that Morrison was upstairs in his room, and I led the way. The secretary's relief at seeing Holmes was clear. 'Thank Heaven you could get down here, Mr Holmes!' said Morrison. 'I yield to no man in my admiration for Inspector Forrester and his constables, worthy fellows all, but the police do have their set procedures, and what I wish for above all else is discretion. I do not know if you are aware of it, sir, but some of the men who stay here are illustrious indeed. Some have an international reputation in their own field, as you might imagine ... why, we have had men staying here who have been knighted for their literary or artistic endeavours. And equally, some of them are known in society by virtue of their birth and position ... we had the brother of a cabinet minister here last week ... thank Heaven he was not here *this* week!'

'Thank Heaven, indeed!' murmured Holmes.

Morrison managed a smile. 'You think that perhaps I am behaving in a melodramatic fashion?' said he. 'I am perhaps a touch over-sensitive as to my position here, but really, Mr Holmes, I do not exaggerate when I say that any breath of scandal would have ramifications far beyond my own humble post.'

'I quite understand,' said Holmes. 'And you may rest assured that I shall do no more than is necessary to arrive at a rapid and discreet solution.'

'Thank you, sir,' said Morrison. 'It goes without saying that you have the run of the place so far as I am concerned. The guests' rooms are, of course, another matter; I have no authority to allow you access to them.'

'It may not be necessary,' said Holmes. 'If there is any difficulty in that direction, then of course the police will have to be brought into the matter, but we will seek to do what we can without any unpleasantness in the first instance.'

'That is all I can ask. I take it you will be staying here?' said Morrison. 'I have arranged a room for you … rather cramped, I fear, as it is a sort of box room by rights, but it was that or the room lately occupied by poor Benjamin Morgan, and I naturally thought …'

'I am sure your choice will be excellent,' said Holmes. 'If I might leave my bag in the room, and then take a look round … Morgan's room first, I think, and then the room where the crime took place?'

Morrison showed Holmes his room, which was not so cramped as the secretary had suggested, and then led the way to another door, which he unlocked.

'All is as it was,' said he. 'The police have had a look round, of course, but no-one else has been in.'

'That is a blessing!' murmured Holmes sadly.

Morrison made as if to lead the way into the room, but Holmes held up a hand. 'I am sure you have better things to do,' said he. 'Watson and I are perfectly accustomed to working alone. Might I have the key? I shall, of course, return it to you, and you may be sure that I shall not hesitate to consult you in case of need.' And with that, he moved swiftly inside the door. Morrison seemed nonplussed for a moment, then nodded and went off back to his own room.

'Right, Watson,' said Holmes, moving aside to allow me in. 'We shall take a quick look round, although I fear that the passage of time and the presence of an official throng will have conspired to render our task useless.'

'What are we seeking?' said I.

'Anything out of the ordinary.'

We looked, but there was nothing untoward. The only thing of interest I noticed was a photograph of a woman, past the first blush of youth, and striking rather than conventionally attractive in appearance, by the bedside.

'His wife, I take it,' said Holmes. 'It is a fine photograph.'

'He was, of course, a portrait photographer,' said I. 'Probably took it himself … if he did so, it is no wonder he had a considerable reputation for his work.'

'H'mm. Nothing else? There are no personal letters, you see.'

'No, but then he was on holiday. He probably dealt with his correspondence before leaving home, and never thought to have his post redirected here. I did exactly the same,' said I.

'Very likely. Well, there seems nothing here to point us in the direction of the truth, so shall we view the scene of the crime?'

He locked the door after us, and I led the way downstairs, and into the dining room.

'Now, Watson,' said Holmes, rubbing his hands with some eagerness, 'to work! Where was the body discovered?'

'In here,' I said, leading the way. 'You see there is a little porch affair, an old doorway to the original house, as I would judge, and it was there that the crime took place.'

'Ah, a telephone!' said Holmes, shaking his head. 'You may recall, Doctor, that I have had my doubts about the advisability of opening one's door to the instrument.'

'Really, Holmes! You surely cannot blame the telephone for what happened?'

'Think you not? And yet, Watson, there may be deep significance in this location, may there not? In the fact that the telephone is here, where the murder took place?'

'How so?'

'Well, Doctor, consider this possibility. This man, Morgan, discovers some heinous crime in commission, or about to be committed. His first thought is naturally to inform the police. The house is isolated, he cannot easily reach the local bobby ... but wait! He has seen the telephone, and knows that the local police station is also likely to have the instrument. He comes in here, to pass on what he knows, but the criminal finds out that Morgan knows something, and pursues him. Morgan enters the cubicle, but the criminal, desperate to avoid detection, pulls open the door, and ...' and he stabbed viciously at the empty air.

'You think that is what happened?' I asked.

'Not for a moment. But it is certainly one explanation, is it not? The sort of thing which ... albeit unlikely ... just may have occurred.' He stared at the interior of the porch. 'Watson, Watson! I had such hopes of Forrester! But the best of them will not learn to leave things alone! Why has the inside been cleaned?'

'Well, Holmes, the ordinary business of the house ... it would have been rather gruesome ... and in any event, a thorough search was made, so Forrester assured me.'

'Indeed?' Holmes stared at the telephone for a time. 'It occurs to me that we may have a clue in our hands at the outset. Had Morgan made a telephone call and hung up, or was he killed before he could lift the receiver?'

'The exchange would know!' I said.

'Indeed, and we must ask without delay.' Holmes was about to lift the receiver, when he was interrupted by Inspector Forrester entering the room.

'Mr Holmes, delighted to see you again, sir. Though I could wish that it were under happier circumstances,' said Forrester.

'As could I. Why did you say that the porch might be cleaned?' asked Holmes sharply.

46

'It had been subjected to a scrupulous examination, sir, and it could hardly be left as it was. Not that there was too much amiss, a little blood on the floor, nothing more. But it would not have been proper to leave it like that. You have my solemn assurance that there was nothing of importance there.'

'H'mm. Well, I shall have to take your word for it, Inspector. Watson here has just remarked that the exchange could tell us whether Morgan had in fact made a telephone call before he was killed.'

'The point had struck me, sir,' said Forrester. 'I asked this morning, and the girl at the exchange remembered that there were but two calls from the house yesterday afternoon, and on both occasions the caller was trying a London number ... the same number in each case ... which did not reply. That would have been Mr Gregson, from my enquiries.'

'A pity. I had hoped that Morgan's call might have told us something. I suppose there is no means of knowing to whom he had intended to speak?'

'Not without a crystal ball, Mr Holmes. I had thought the same ... indeed, I had entertained a sort of wild hope that Mr Morgan might have been speaking on the telephone when ... when it happened, and that the person on the other end might have told us something. But, if he never made his call, then we are in the realms of guesswork.'

'As you say, Inspector. Has there been a full post-mortem dissection of the body?'

'There has, sir, but there was nothing to alter the opinion which the police surgeon and Dr Watson here had already formed ... death caused by a single stab wound to the heart, and the weapon left in the wound.'

'You have the weapon here?'

'Yes, sir.' Forrester produced a silk handkerchief, in which was wrapped the letter opener I had seen yesterday, the stains on it now a dull rust colour.

Holmes examined it carefully with his lens. 'There is a finger mark here,' said he.

(I may add that finger marks were what is called 'all the rage' at that time. There were even moves afoot to establish a

47

Fingerprint Bureau at Scotland Yard, although it was not actually set up until a couple of years after the case of which I am writing.)

'Yes, sir,' said Forrester, 'that is the mark of Mr Gregson's index finger. One of my men has a turn for scientific detection, and he examined the mark. He's a keen sort of chap, Mr Holmes, and I'm sure that even you would approve of his methods. He also told me that the smudges you see there "might be anything".'

'I would concur there,' said Holmes with a smile. 'And I am sure that his opinion of the clearer mark is correct.'

'It does not help much, though,' I pointed out, 'for you might reasonably expect a man's own finger marks to be seen on his own letter opener.'

'True enough, Watson,' said Holmes.

'Well, Mr Holmes,' said Forrester, 'if there's nothing more I can do?'

'I think not, Inspector. I shall inform you if I find anything out. You have formed no opinion yourself?'

'Only that things look very bad against Mr Gregson, sir. Could I but find a motive, I might be tempted to put the handcuffs on him.'

'He seemed genuinely upset last night,' I said. 'If his distress were feigned, then he is the best actor I have ever seen ... yourself not excepted, Holmes.'

'And he was upset at finding the body yesterday, according to the gardener,' added Forrester.

'You are both quite convinced, then?' said Holmes.

'Are you not?' said Forrester.

'Well, he might truly be the best actor the world has ever seen!'

'Really, Holmes!' I said. 'Be he never so brilliant an actor, it would surely have occurred to him that a safer course of action ... were he the murderer ... would be to sneak out quietly and unobserved.'

'A touch, Watson! But then he could not guarantee that he would be unobserved ... he might have been seen leaving the dining room, and then what chance would he have of escaping justice? I believe that you told me yesterday evening that he had bloodstained trousers?'

'The blood got there when the body fell against him,' said Forrester. 'Or so he claims.'

'Or so he claims. But what if the blood got there when he stabbed Morgan? Gregson looks down, sees the stains which he knows will incriminate him. What can he do? Under different circumstances he might wash the trousers, or burn them. But he is not at home ... the kitchen is occupied by curious servants, and similarly if he were to order a fire lit in his room on a hot summer's day, there would certainly be talk amongst the maids, and then questions to answer later. A clever man might conclude that the safest course of action was the boldest, and pretend to having found the body. His shouts of terror might have been intended to lend verisimilitude ... after all, who suspects a frightened man?'

'A clever man indeed!' said I, 'for he must needs have thought it out fast ... damned fast. Remember that he would have had to decide on such a course of action on the spur of the moment. He did not have the time ... as you have had the time, Holmes ... to sit and think the problem through over a pipe or two of Bradley's strongest.'

Holmes laughed in his peculiar noiseless fashion. 'You are right, as always, Watson. A clever man indeed! Or a bold man,' he added thoughtfully.

'Or a desperate man?' suggested Forrester.

'A madman?' I contributed.

Holmes stared at me. 'I confess I had not considered that possibility fully, Watson. Yet it is not without consequence, for I understand that there is evidence to show that no strangers approached the house from outside?'

Forrester nodded. 'The gardeners were outside the whole time,' said he. 'They are good chaps ... just working men, of course, but honest enough ... and they are none of them involved with the house, or anyone inside it.'

'In which case, be Gregson the murderer or no, the real murderer was ... and still is ... inside the house,' said Holmes.

'I had worked that out myself, sir,' said Forrester. 'I'll confess that Dr Watson is a braver man than I am, to stay here last night knowing what he did know.'

'Oh, I locked my door!' said I. 'And took a hefty ash stick to bed with me, in the absence of any better weapon.'

'That reminds me,' said Holmes, taking my old revolver from his pocket and handing it to me. 'I trust you may not need it, but better safe than sorry. It's this way,' he went on, 'if the murderer had some reason for his crime, if he intended to kill Morgan and nobody else, then the house is safe enough, all we have to concern ourselves with is tracking the killer down. But if the murderer is indeed a madman, as Watson has suggested, or if Morgan were not the only man against whom the murderer has some grievance, whether real or imagined, then there may be further unpleasantness to come.'

'You take that possibility seriously?' asked Forrester.

'It is a possibility,' said Holmes. 'Although I have some hopes that the police interest in the case, and ... dare I say it? ... the presence of Watson and myself in the house, may help to prevent further mischief, if indeed any such had been projected. But it is clear that the murderer ... unless he really were that madman whom Watson has postulated ... must have had, or at any rate thought he had, some grievance against Morgan. And as we have said, it may be that the murderer has, or believes he has, some grievance against one or more of the other men who are staying here. That being so, it is very necessary that we should question the occupants of the house to determine their various relations with one another.'

'Then I shall leave you to it,' said Forrester, and after the usual civilities he suited the action to the words, and Holmes and I were alone in the dining room once more.

'Now, Watson, let us start in good earnest. You have some acquaintance with the men here, and I do not. Where shall we begin?'

'Morrison, the secretary, asked them all not to go too far from the house until you had seen each of them, so they should all be somewhere close to hand. Perhaps we should look in the sitting room, for they are probably in there, or some of them at least.'

I led the way to the sitting room. It was empty save for Lane, who sat in a chair by the French window scribbling in his notebook. He rose to greet us as we entered.

'Ah,' said he, holding out his hand, 'this must be the famous Mr Sherlock Holmes.'

I believe that I have already remarked on Lane's cynical sense of humour. There was something of that in his greeting, but I thought I could detect another element as well – might it be envy, perhaps? Or could it possibly be – fear?

However, Holmes did not appear to notice anything out of the ordinary, and murmured the usual courtesies. 'I imagine that you and Dr Watson get on famously,' Holmes added, 'since you are both literary men.'

Lane laughed. 'I fear that I rather shocked Dr Watson last night, by revealing that I contemplated writing some account of this sad business for publication.'

'Ah!' said Holmes, 'you must not mind Watson! He is so used to having it all his own way when it comes to furnishing the reading public with tales of my doings. It may perhaps be no bad thing to have a fresh approach. Indeed, I have on occasion been obliged to criticize Watson for his emphasis on the more sensational aspects of the various problems with which I have been associated.'

From the look on Lane's face, I could tell that this was a blow – he had evidently been counting on those 'sensational aspects' in large measure to provide the material for his proposed book. For the rest, I was in no sense offended by Holmes's remarks, for I was well enough aware that he intended merely to win Lane's confidence, so that the ensuing interview might go the easier.

'If I might have just a very few words?' said Holmes.

'Mr Morrison asked us to tell you anything you wished to know,' said Lane. 'I must say, it is something of a novelty to be a suspect in a murder investigation. Quite thrilling, in fact.'

'I hardly think that we shall consider you very seriously as a suspect,' said Holmes with a laugh. 'After all, I understand that this was your first visit to the house, so you had ... presumably ... never met Morgan before?'

'Ah, but you cannot be sure,' said Lane, with more confidence than he had hitherto shown. 'How do you know, Mr Holmes, that I am not Morgan's long-lost nephew, come back from foreign parts to murder him and claim my inheritance?'

'You may be sure that I shall look closely even into that remote possibility,' said Holmes calmly. 'By the by, you are not Morgan's long-lost nephew, or anything of that sort, are you?'

'Indeed, no!' said Lane, obviously impressed by Holmes's demeanour. 'I was merely trying to show that the solution to the puzzle may not be the obvious one.'

'It was very kind of you to point that out, and you may be quite sure that I shall bear it firmly in mind,' said Holmes. 'Now, I imagine that you have yourself done a little in the way of looking into the problem, even in the short time since the murder took place. So perhaps you would favour us with any theories you may have formed, or any information you have unearthed.'

Lane looked at him in some surprise. 'Why, yes! I don't know how you knew, but you are right, I have done a little looking about.' He leaned back in his chair, evidently flattered that Holmes had seen fit to consult him. 'How, in general terms, do you imagine the crime was committed?'

'Well, in very general terms, I understand that the murderer probably came through the house into the dining room, opened the door to the porch, and ... did the deed.'

'So the police think,' said Lane. 'But the murderer could equally well have approached the porch from the outside, through the garden.'

'But I understood that there was someone in the garden the whole time?' said Holmes.

'So it was said. But I have discovered that there was a short time ... at the right time, for the murderer ... when the back garden was empty. By the way,' he asked, 'can a garden be described as empty? I mean, of course, that there was nobody out there ... unless, of course, the murderer happened to be out there.'

'Indeed?' said Holmes. 'That is contrary to my information.'

'I imagine it is,' said Lane, a smug smile on his face. 'At around three o'clock, Welsh and his assistant came to the house for a cup of tea. Welsh stayed inside, as you know, and the lad went back out. But ... and I discovered this only this morning by talking to Welsh ... the lad had occasion to answer a call of nature. He used the domestic offices by the side of the house, then went to the kitchen to wash his hands, and only then did he take his cup of tea outside.'

'He cannot have been away from the garden for very long, surely?' said I.

Lane shrugged. 'Five minutes? Perhaps ten? Who can say? But, be the time never so short, for a time he was not outside, and thus could not observe the back of the house.'

'That is something I did not know,' said Holmes. 'It illustrates once again the inadvisability of taking things for granted. Yes, the police ... not to speak of Watson and myself ... ought to have enquired as to that.'

'Even so,' said I, stung slightly by the implied criticism, 'I cannot see that it alters matters very much. After all, if the murderer did approach via the garden, then he would have been obliged to wait until the men were out of the way. He could not possibly guarantee that Morgan would actually be inside the porch at the time in question. Nor could he legitimately rely on the state of the assistant gardener's digestive tract! The lad might well have been back outside immediately, and then the murderer would have been in trouble, with a vengeance.'

'The point is a valid one,' said Holmes.

Lane said, 'But the objection is not insuperable. If the murderer knew the ways of the house, he would know that Welsh went for his tea at three o'clock each day ... regular as clockwork ... I noticed that myself last week. What more natural than to assume ... albeit incorrectly ... that the assistant would do precisely the same? Welsh is frequently indoors for five or ten minutes. Not always, I agree, but often enough. The murderer may well have assumed that he had a clear run for that ten minutes ... ten minutes in which to commit his crime.'

'H'mm. That may well be so,' said Holmes. 'Of course, there is another, and more powerful, objection to all this.'

'Indeed?' asked Lane.

'You do not see it? No matter. Now, I must ask you this ... where were you at three o'clock yesterday afternoon?'

Lane looked shamefaced. 'I was in the library.'

'Which is right next door to the dining room?'

Lane nodded, without speaking.

'And yet you heard nothing?' asked Holmes.

'The fact is, I was a little sleepy after luncheon yesterday ... it was curried chicken, one of my particular favourites, and I had a generous portion ... so I went in there to rest for a moment or two. I succeeded so well that I fell asleep.'

'Only think,' I could not help myself saying, 'had you been awake and alert, you might have caught the murderer red-handed! Or even prevented the crime! That would be something to write a book about!'

'I scarcely think that amusing, sir,' said Lane coldly.

'Indeed not! Most unseemly!' said Holmes, adding rather mischievously, 'And if the murderer had been interrupted or discovered, who can say but that there may not have been two victims instead of one?'

'Good God!' said Lane. 'I never thought of that! Thank Heaven for that second helping of curry!'

'Your presence in the library, awake or not, does tend to confirm that the murderer did not approach from the garden,' Holmes remarked thoughtfully. 'After all, he could not be certain that the library was unoccupied, or that any occupant might be dozing. For that matter,' he added, getting to his feet and walking over to the French window, which stood open in the heat, 'the murderer could not be sure that there would be no-one in this room. I observe that there is a very limited view of the garden from the chairs in here, but by walking through this window and proceeding only a couple of paces ...' and he did just that as he spoke ... 'a man may obtain a fine prospect of the entire garden.'

'Tomlinson was in here yesterday afternoon,' volunteered Lane. 'And Pountney was upstairs in his room, which also commands a view of the garden at this side of the house. Or at least, that is where they claim to have been.'

'What, indoors on a hot day like yesterday?' said Holmes. 'Still, it does lend yet more weight to the theory that the murderer approached from inside the house.'

'You mean it was one of them? Or should I say, "one of us", perhaps?' said Lane.

'I did not say so.'

Lane stood up. 'If there is nothing more, Mr Holmes? I could do with a little fresh air, to clear my head.'

'Nothing more for the time being, sir,' said Holmes.

Lane nodded to us, and went out through the French window into the garden.

'Well Watson?' asked Holmes, when Lane was out of earshot.

'One of the guests described him as an impertinent puppy, or something of that sort, yesterday,' said I, 'and I am bound to say that I concur entirely with that view. That apart, there are a couple of interesting points. First of all, Lane's discovery that there was no-one outside for a short while alters matters quite considerably, does it not?'

'It certainly alters them slightly.'

'More than slightly, I should say, Holmes. We have assumed that no outsider … a tramp, or gypsy, or something of that sort … could have killed Morgan. But, if there were nobody in the garden at the time in question, then such an unknown assailant might well have reached the house unobserved.'

'It is indeed a point,' said Holmes, 'but not as significant as you seem to think, Watson. For one thing, a tramp or a gypsy might very well come up to the house to steal, but surely not to kill? Why should a stranger kill Morgan, unless it were in the heat of the moment, if, shall we say, Morgan had interrupted him in his pilfering? And that seems unlikely … your convenient unknown itinerant would lurk outside the house, and Morgan was inside. For another thing … more significant yet … there is the problem of the weapon. I understand that Gregson claims it was upstairs, in his room? Well, then, how came it to be downstairs in the first place? The very fact of its being used as a weapon has ... quite understandably ... overshadowed the equally important fact of its being removed from Gregson's room at all.'

'I never thought of that! Why, if we could find who took it from the room, we might also find the murderer!' And, being somewhat unwilling to abandon my own theory, I added, 'An outsider might have taken it, though, and used it to kill Morgan when he tried to prevent the thief leaving the house!'

'Hardly, Watson! That would mean that the thief must have entered the house before either Gregson or Morgan went into the porch to use the telephone, and we know that is out of the question, for Welsh and his fellows were outside earlier. But you are right in saying that if we could find the man who took the letter opener, we might go a long a way towards solving the mystery. Bear in mind, Watson, that a man who steals one item may well steal others. Has anything else been taken from any of the rooms, I wonder?'

'Nobody has said as much. But then the lamentable events of yesterday afternoon have, as you say, put everything else in the shade.'

'Let us imagine for a moment that one of the guests is a thief.'

'Holmes!'

'Merely for the sake of argument, my dear fellow. He enters Gregson's room, takes the silver letter opener, perhaps other desirable items, and leaves the room. Morgan sees him leaving. Now, if the thief had an armful of swag, of course Morgan would be immediately suspicious. But if the thief had stowed his booty in his pockets ... small, but valuable items ... then Morgan might think that the thief had been in Gregson's room legitimately, to smoke a cigar with Gregson, say, or that he had looked in to say that he was off to the village and to ask if he could carry out any small commission for Gregson, that kind of thing. In a place like this, the guests ... and especially if they know one another well ... probably look in on one another two or three times a day.'

'True enough. Morgan might not suspect anything immediately, but the thief would know that as soon as Gregson raised the alarm about the theft, then at that point Morgan would recall what he had seen.'

Holmes nodded.

'So, your first theory about Morgan's being killed to prevent his telling what he knew might be correct!' said I. 'Still, it does seem a big step, Holmes, from what is frankly little more than petty theft to murder. Were I ... Heaven forbid! ... ever in such reduced circumstances that I must steal from my acquaintances, then if I feared discovery I would not kill and face the noose. Instead, I should stuff my pockets with the most valuable plunder, and clear off, take the first train out of the place, lose myself in the crowds of London with a false beard and a false name.'

'That is one obvious objection. You had other points to raise, I believe?'

'Indeed, I had. I shall trade you information for information. In the first place, everyone says that Gregson kicked up a considerable fuss when he found Morgan's body. How came Lane to sleep through the noise, two helpings of curry notwithstanding?'

'Well done! I had wondered about that myself.'

'And then, did you notice Lane's behaviour when you first came in here?'

'Oh, you felt that, too, then? Yes, Watson, I seemed to note a rather curious demeanour. But that does not necessarily imply guilt. An innocent man confronted by the forces of the law may well feel unsettled.'

'Rather as a man may dread a visit to his dentist, though he knows perfectly well that his teeth are sound?'

'Your parallel is exact,' said Holmes, laughing. 'No, I would not attach too much importance to his bearing, were that all. After all, even an older man, a man of the world, may well feel upset at such a dramatic event as murder. Lane is young, he is a stranger here, among older men, men whom he does not know, men who have perhaps offered him a cigar, played billiards with him, told him tall stories. It would not be too unbelievable if the thought of one of those men being a murderer unsettled him, now would it? But your first point, about his sleeping through the noise made by Gregson, is, as you say, most interesting. I feel strongly that there is something we have not seen yet, something we have not been told, perhaps, and we shall keep Mr Lane in mind. Now, what would you have me tell you in exchange?'

'Really, Holmes!' said I. 'You know very well! First of all, how did you know that Lane would have been making enquiries?'

'There is no mystery there. He plans a book about what has happened. What more natural than that he should do a little research on his own account? The urge to amateur detection is quite irresistible! And understandable ... after all, if he could solve the crime himself, that would do sales of his book no harm, now would it? You surely do not tell me, Watson, that you yourself had no such aspirations before I got here?'

'Certainly not!' said I, adding hastily, 'Well, then, what was the objection to the murderer's approaching from the garden, the objection which Lane failed to see, and which you glossed over?'

'Ah, yes, now that is a little more to the point. And, of course, you mentioned it yourself, in passing.'

'Indeed?'

'Indeed. Do you not recall the circumstance?'

'For Heaven's sake, Holmes!'

'Well, then. Tell me, Watson, you examined the outer door of the porch pretty thoroughly, did you not?'

'Pretty thoroughly, Holmes.'

'Describe it to me.'

'Oak, heavy oak, old, black, three inches thick. Perhaps a couple of hundred years old. Heavy iron latch, and a modern ... and effective ... Chubb lock. Oh, and studded on the outside with square-headed iron nails, for decorative effect.'

Holmes clapped his hands. 'Excellent! Oh ... any window?'

'Oh, of course, I forgot ... four tiny panes, set high up. Odd glass, old ... I can't remember what you call it ... like the bottom of a glass bottle. Greenish-grey, practically opaque. Useless for illumination.'

'And worse for seeing through?'

'Absolutely! But ... Good God, Holmes!'

'You see, Watson?'

'I see ... where the murderer could not, or at least not from the garden.'

'Where the murderer could not,' repeated Holmes slowly. 'You said yourself that the murderer could not guarantee Morgan's presence in the porch ... I would go further, and say that the murderer could not even be aware of it! If the murderer had been in the garden, he cannot have been up near the house, or the gardeners would have seen him. Therefore, he must have been at the far end, where it is quite overgrown. He would have seen Gregson go in from the garden using the outer door, but could not have seen him leave ... and Morgan enter ... via the inner door and the dining room. The only way you could see that is through the French window in the corner of the dining room ... and even then, you would have to stand at the side of the house near the kitchen door. You must approach the house, and the kitchen door, so closely that you must be seen by the occupants of the kitchen.'

'And the same applies to anyone looking out from the house,' said I. 'They would also see Gregson come in from the garden, but not go out through the dining room.'

'An excellent point,' said Holmes. 'So that even if the murderer did approach the porch through the house, as we have thought, it may still have been the case ...'

'That he thought Gregson was still inside the porch!'

Holmes nodded. 'And certainly anyone looking at the house from the garden must have thought that.'

'But, Holmes! If your theory is correct ...' I stopped, my head whirling.

'Yes, Doctor?'

'If Gregson were the intended victim, and not Morgan ... why, that means that the murderer failed!'

Holmes nodded.

'But then he might try again, Holmes!'

'He might indeed, Doctor.'

'But should we not tell Gregson this?'

'Tell me what?'

I glanced up in some considerable surprise, and perhaps even with a muttered imprecation, for it was Gregson himself, looking pale and drawn, who had just entered the room. He threw himself wearily into an armchair, and asked again, 'Tell me what?'

Four

'And for that matter,' Gregson asked Holmes, 'who might you be?'

'My name is Sherlock Holmes.'

'Ah, yes, the renowned private detective of Baker Street. We were informed that you had been summoned, and here you are! Well, sir, you might have saved yourself a fatiguing journey,' said Gregson, recovering his spirits somewhat, 'for the police think I did the foul deed ... and everyone in the house seems to agree with 'em. Not that I can blame them, I must say. Why, if I didn't know for certain that I was innocent, I'm damned if I wouldn't suspect myself!'

'I can assure you, sir,' said Holmes, 'that I have not jumped to any such conclusion, and nor has Dr Watson.'

'And you wouldn't say as much if you had, in any case, eh? After all, if you let on that you suspected me, I might attack you ... I haven't got a knife about me at the moment, but I could do some damage with this ...' and he waved a hunk of bread at us as he spoke. Subsiding slightly, and sounding rather ashamed of himself, he added, 'You will excuse my manners, gentlemen, but I am under somewhat of a strain just at the moment. Excuse also my informal meal ... but I simply could not face the accusing looks at breakfast, and I was famished. I wheedled this from Mrs Welsh ... she is a good soul, though somewhat limited in her outlook. Indeed, she is perhaps the only one in the house who does not think me a murderer, or a madman, or both.'

'I think it quite likely that you are the innocent victim of circumstances,' said Holmes calmly. 'But in order to convince the police of that, I must present them with the real culprit, and that necessitates asking some few questions of the various guests in the house, yourself included.'

Gregson nodded, and said through a mouthful of bread, 'I see that. Fire away, sir!'

Holmes threw his cigarette case to Gregson. 'You seem in need of a sedative, so help yourself. Now, how long had you known the murdered man?'

'About half my life, or a little longer,' said Gregson, wiping away a stray crumb, then lighting a cigarette and blowing out an enormous cloud of blue smoke.

'Indeed? I had formed the impression that you met here, for some reason.'

'Not at all. As a matter of fact, we went to art school together. We were never close friends, don't ask me why ... there was no sort of active hostility, not then, we just moved in different circles.'

'You said "not then". There was what you called "active hostility" later, though?'

Gregson looked somewhat ashamed. 'There were some discussions as to what exactly constituted "Art" and what did not. Those sometimes became a little ... and more than a little ... acrimonious.'

'H'mm. Acrimonious or no, it certainly seems a very trivial *casus belli*,' said Holmes.

Gregson gave an indifferent shrug of his shoulders. 'Not worth killing for, you mean? I would quite agree with you there.'

'Come, sir,' said Holmes. 'We are all men of the world. Unless you are forthright with me, I can hardly be expected to help you ... for I will tell you frankly that it seems that the police do entertain some suspicions of you. And this childish nonsense as to what may or may not be "Art" hardly seems a reason for murder.'

Gregson shrugged his shoulders again.

'You have come under suspicion, and for murder,' said Holmes again. 'If you are arrested, tried and found guilty, I need not remind you of the penalty which the law exacts. If you are innocent, you have nothing to fear from me.'

Gregson looked suitably abashed, but still hesitated before he spoke. 'It is an old tale,' he said at last. 'And a sordid enough tale, in all conscience. I fear it may shock you, for all your worldly pretensions.'

'You had best let us be the judges of that,' said Holmes.

'Very well. But remember that I tried to warn you.' Gregson drew on his cigarette, and blew out a great cloud of smoke. 'We were both young men, Benjamin Morgan and I, at the very threshold of our respective careers. Perhaps not exactly starving in the proverbial garret, but not so very far away from it at times. There was an art dealer, a lady ... dead now, I fear, but her name might at one time have been familiar even to you ... and she had a small but exclusive gallery in London. Her shows were famous throughout the country, and abroad. Mostly the exhibitors were equally famous, names of some consequence in artistic circles. It chanced that between two of these notable displays there was a gap in the calendar, and she bethought herself to encourage a young, struggling artist. Quite by chance she narrowed the choice down to Ben Morgan and myself ... and I emphasize that it was by chance, for, as I told you, we were never close, and by that time we had quite lost touch. Now, there could be but one exhibition, and there were two artists ... the gallery was scarcely big enough to display work by both of us. So, was it to be the progressive sculptor, or the brilliant photographer? It was difficult to choose on the basis of our work, and so the lady decided to apply another criterion.' He drew on his cigarette.

Holmes raised an eyebrow. 'Yes?'

'Oh, dear!' sighed Gregson. 'Are you really so naive? Well, then ... the lady's customers collected works of art. The lady herself, however, had other tastes. She collected young men. Do I positively need to elaborate?'

'Indeed, no!' said I, fervently.

Gregson gave a wry smile, and smoked in silence for a time.

'That is surely not the whole of your story?' prompted Holmes.

'Not quite. The lady's choice fell first on Ben. We never spoke of it, but I imagine she put it to him fairly bluntly ... certainly she put it to me fairly bluntly, when it came to my turn. Ben refused; I did not. I got the exhibition, and it set my career off in a modestly spectacular fashion.'

I could not think of anything to say to this odd and somewhat disturbing revelation; but Holmes merely remarked, 'If you never spoke of it to Morgan, how came you to know that he had been ... approached, shall we say?'

Gregson looked most downcast. 'Oh, there can be no doubt.'

'But ...'

'If you must know, the lady herself told me, in a ... what I might call a tender moment.'

'Ah, I see.'

Gregson waved Holmes's cigarette case in the air. 'May I be further indebted to you?'

'Please do.'

Gregson lit another cigarette, and threw the case over to Holmes. 'Thank you, sir. And of course, once I got the show, Ben would know just what had been going on, would know what price I had had to pay.' He leaned forward and spoke earnestly. 'But don't you see, Mr Holmes, that although that rather sordid old episode might account for the strained relations between Morgan and myself, it was the wrong way round?'

Holmes looked a question at him.

'It was I, and not Ben, who ... well, let us be plain, who put my career before my conscience. It was my career, not his, which benefited from my ungentlemanly conduct. I can see that Ben might resent that ... although I do not in all honesty think that he would resent it enough to want to kill me because of it ... but why on earth should I want to kill him because of it? It is, as I say, the wrong way round; it simply makes no sense.'

'Then what does?' asked Holmes. 'What reason would anyone have for killing Morgan?'

Gregson shook his head. 'There you find me at a complete loss, Mr Holmes. I do not think that any of the men in the house felt even the kind of petty dislike ... and, in truth, how very petty it now seems! ... that I once felt. We had grown ... I will not say we had grown closer with time ... but we had, I think, grown to respect one another's work as we grew older. Perhaps we had simply begun to grow up, belatedly enough in all conscience.'

'What did you know of his private life?'

'Only that it was exceptionally private. He would hardly speak of intimate matters to me, even latterly, given what the relations between us had once been, but I do not think he ever confided in any of the others either, though they got on with him better than I.'

'Was he married, say? Did you know that much?'

'Married? No.' Gregson hesitated. 'Not as such.'

'Oh?'

'He had his own standards, you see. The artistic temperament, once again! He has often spoken about marriage in harsh terms, said that the marriage certificate is the death warrant for a woman's freedom, that sort of thing. I could go along with much of what he said, but some of it was pretty radical. But that was Benjamin Morgan for you ... you might not agree with all his views, but you could never doubt his sincerity.'

'The police will, I imagine, have informed the lady concerned?'

'Not unless they're damned clever,' said Gregson bluntly, 'for I know for a fact that she is on the Continent, somewhere between Italy and Greece. A sketching tour of sorts. Ben came here, she went there.'

'She is evidently of independent views too,' said Holmes. 'An artist in her own right, I take it?'

'In an amateur way only,' said Gregson. 'The sort of genteel, delicate watercolour studies of flowers in which a certain class of genteel, delicate English lady tends to specialize. I have seen a few of them. They ... well, as I say, she is an artist in an amateur way only.'

'And have you also seen the lady, as well as her sketches?'

Gregson shook his head. 'Never. I tell you, Ben kept his private life very private.'

'And if she is not an artist, then what does she do?'

'Keeps house for Ben, I imagine. Is that not what they all end up doing? The presence or absence of a wedding ring never seems to alter the actual status quo, does it?'

'Well,' said Holmes, 'if the lady is abroad, she can scarcely be a factor in the murder.' He frowned. 'And by the same token, it cannot have been the lady whom Morgan was trying to contact on the telephone. You would not venture a guess as to whom he might have been trying to reach?'

'I would not. It might have been anyone … except the lady in question, of course. It must obviously have been someone who has a telephone, so that would narrow the field. A banker, or stockbroker, would you not think? Someone of that sort?'

'You are probably right,' said Holmes. 'And your own telephone call?'

'Oh, there is no mystery there. I am to have an exhibition … the outstanding events in my life seem to coincide with exhibitions! And with lady gallery owners, for it is a lady who is arranging this exhibition, too. You need have no fear that I am about to shock you,' he added with a smile, 'for she is married to a very worthy lawyer. Very worthy, and very dull, too, but dull as he is, she loves him very much. I know that, because I offered her the chance to leave him. Oh, dear! Now I have shocked you!'

'Not at all,' said Holmes untruthfully. 'Pray continue.'

'Her own gallery was too small to take my sculptures, so she was obliged to hire rooms. At the last moment, there was some difficulty, some quibble over the terms, and there seemed every prospect that the arrangements might have to be cancelled. I worry about occurrences of that kind, I always have done. So, I wanted to speak to Sarah … the lady concerned … and rang her accordingly. But there was no reply.'

'And this was at three o'clock?'

'No, this was earlier, when luncheon was just over. Around two o'clock, or so. I let myself out of the house and into the garden, closing the door, but not locking it ... the key was on the inside. I knew that I should be wanting to get back in to try again, you see. I had taken a canvas and sketch pad and so on outside earlier, to make a few drawings of the house ... I draw partly as a break from sculpting, and also to record ideas for my statues. I tried, but could not settle, not with the uneasiness about the possible failure of the exhibition. But I stuck at it, until Welsh ... who had been working close by me, near the little round pond out there ... walked past and said it was tea time, or words to that effect.

'I looked at my watch, and was rather surprised to find that an hour or so had passed. I had intended to try the telephone a little earlier, but had not done so, and now I saw that it was almost exactly three. I stood up, said "Hullo", or something of the kind, to Welsh and his assistant, then went inside and tried Sarah again. There was still no reply, and I was undecided what to do. Just then, I heard the main door of the dining room open, so I opened the inner door, and there was Morgan, just come into the room. He said "Sorry", or something, as you do, and made as if to leave, but I told him that I had finished, and held the door open for him. I myself went into the dining room. I wanted to try the telephone again, but you will understand that I did not want to hang around whilst Morgan was speaking on the instrument, and so I went to the front door to smoke a cigarette.'

'Now,' said Holmes, 'you said that the two gardeners passed you as you initially went to the outer door?'

'I am certain of that, for I spoke to them. They will tell you the same, I am sure.'

'I did not question that,' said Holmes. 'But the point is of the first importance, for there has been a suggestion that some unknown person might have approached the outer door of the porch via the garden, as the two men were both inside for some short time ... Welsh to drink his tea, the lad to use the domestic offices before he went back to the garden.'

Gregson shook his head. 'I think you may safely eliminate that theory, Mr Holmes. Even if the assistant gardener were inside for some considerable time, so too was I. As I have told you, I was concerned about the state of my forthcoming exhibition. I therefore remained at the telephone for some quite considerable time, letting it ring in the hope of an answer. The girl at the exchange would, I am sure, confirm that, were you to ask her. Indeed,' he added with a smile, 'I am quite certain that she will remember, for she told me more than once that there was no reply, and asked ... rather pointedly ... if I wished her to continue trying.'

'So, it is your opinion that the assistant gardener would have returned to the garden by the time you left the dining room and Morgan went in?'

'Well, I could not swear to it on oath ... I was inside, and so could not possibly see just when the assistant went back to the garden; but for all practical purposes ... unless his sojourn in the privy were of a duration which would indicate that Dr Watson's professional opinion might be required ... I should say that he must certainly have been back in the garden when I turned the telephone over to Morgan.'

'I see. That is most important,' said Holmes. 'Now, I know this next question will be painful, but could you possibly bring yourself to recount your discovery of the body?'

Gregson shuddered theatrically. 'I shall never forget it, sir! Never! I finished my cigarette, and returned to the dining room. It was all in silence. The inner door to the porch was closed, and at first I did not know if Morgan had gone, or might still be in there. I cleared my throat, to announce my presence, and went nearer the door. There was no sound from inside, so I opened the door, and ...' and he broke off with a sort of sob.

'The body, as I understand it, fell out more or less literally at your feet?'

Gregson nodded, unable to bring himself to speak.

'Now, was the body facing you, or was the back towards you?' asked Holmes.

Gregson stared at him.

'It is of the first importance. It might indicate, you see, which door Morgan had been facing when he was killed ... the knife was in his chest, so he must have been facing his killer. He would naturally look up, turn round, as the door opened ... you follow?'

'Oh, I see.' Gregson stared into space, then waved his hands in the air, as if trying to recreate the circumstances of yesterday afternoon. 'No,' he said at last, 'if you were to press me, I should have to say that the body fell out more or less sideways, as it were.'

Holmes sighed.

'It sort of turned round as it fell, you know,' Gregson elaborated, with every indication of trying to be helpful.

'No matter. It would have been useful to know, but ... no matter.' Holmes thought in silence, then added, 'If only things had been left as they were! An acute observer might still have deduced much!'

'Things were very confused,' Gregson pointed out. 'Our first concern was to see if any spark of life remained, rather than to worry about which way round the body had been.'

'Of course.' Holmes's look spoke volumes. 'It must have been a double shock for you, since of course you would immediately recognize your own letter opener?'

'Indeed, it was.' Gregson's face grew haggard. 'It was up in my room, you know! It really was! I swear it was!'

'I am sure it was,' said Holmes in his most soothing tones. 'You carry it with you always?'

'I have a leather writing case, with paper, envelopes, and what have you. The letter opener is part of the fittings, there is a little leather loop device to hold it. I always take the case when I travel, so I always have the letter opener.'

'I understand. You said "our" first concern was to check the body for signs of life. Who else was in there ... who came into the room to see what had happened?'

'Welsh was the first. I knocked on the kitchen door, and he obviously heard that, or perhaps my shouts ... for I made a fair old din, I think, though I cannot even be certain as to that. He came in through the serving door from the kitchen ... and I was never more glad to see a man in my life, for I simply had no notion as to what to do. Then ... I cannot recall ... yes, Pountney and Tomlinson came along then, together as usual. They more

69

or less took charge, brought Gordon Morrison down, and what have you. They took me out into the library, calmed me down somewhat.'

'We have heard that Tomlinson was in the sitting room,' said Holmes. 'Where was Pountney, think you?'

Gregson shook his head. 'Up in his room, I think. I did not exactly ask, you are to understand, but I got that impression. Yes, when I think about it, for he came down the stairs as Welsh was helping me out of the dining room.'

'He too had heard your calls for help, even upstairs in his room?'

'I think he must have. As I say, I gave voice pretty freely, and hammered on the door.'

'And yet you say they had to go to fetch Morrison down? Did he not hear you, then?'

Gregson frowned. 'He was most probably working, busy at his desk.'

'Of course.'

'Was there anything more?' asked Gregson. 'If not, I should like a breath of fresh air.'

'There is nothing more at the moment,' said Holmes.

Gregson stood up, and went out through the French windows.

'Bit like a stage farce, this,' said I. 'People coming and going through the French windows.'

'Indeed. But there are serious aspects, too, are there not? Tell me, Watson, what is your opinion of Mr Gregson?'

'Lower than it was, Holmes. Why, the fellow openly admits to having been little more than … than a gigolo! And that other business … trying to persuade a respectably married woman to leave her husband! Reminds me of that old tom cat which used to come on to the wall of the back yard and serenade us!'

'The one you discouraged by throwing Sir Henry Baskerville's boot at him? That was a sad loss to my little museum!' Holmes put his hands together, sank his chin on to them, and stared into the air. 'I had a good many difficulties in my early days,' said he, 'but … thank Heaven … I was never offered that particular solution to them!'

'Holmes!'

'But who can say what my response might have been, had the offer ever been made?'

'Holmes!'

'And, indeed, whether I should have proved equal to the task?'

'Really, Holmes!'

He gazed at me reflectively. 'And did not you yourself, in one of your more sensational chronicles, boast of an experience of women which extends over three separate continents?'

'Completely different thing, Holmes! And it has been widely misinterpreted at that! And besides,' I added, 'I wish I had never thought of that damned silly statement! I never heard the last of it from my wife!'

Holmes laughed. 'More to the point,' said he, 'Gregson was at some pains to tell us that it was Morgan who had most cause to bear a grudge. But think, Watson, how would you react to seeing a man who knew that you had a sordid secret such as that hidden in your past? To knowing that he knew the worst of you? Might it not be that a man would brood on that, think he was being despised for his youthful indiscretions, dwell upon it until it warped his mind ... warped it to the extent that the only way to assuage his self-loathing was the removal of what he saw as the personification of his guilty conscience? Yes, there may be possibilities there, though to be sure they are more in the line of your alienist colleagues than of the humble detective.' He suddenly got to his feet. 'Well, Watson, we have heard some account from Gregson as to events inside the house ... if we are to believe him. Now let us see the gardeners, and find out what happened outside.'

Five

As I followed Holmes outside, I said, 'You never got around to telling Gregson that we suspect that the murderer had meant to kill him.'

'No, Watson, and the omission was deliberate. If we have it completely wrong, and Gregson is in fact the man we seek, then it would do no good to tell him our erroneous theory ... indeed, it would merely make him feel more secure in his villainy. If we are wrong in part, and Morgan was in truth the intended victim of some unknown assailant, then again it would be pointless to suggest otherwise.'

'But if we are right, Holmes?'

'If we are right, then it would alert Gregson to any potential danger, true enough, but it would also worry him ... and perhaps unnecessarily at that, for our presence in the house should, as I have said, prevent further attempts. Gregson seems sufficiently upset as it is, without adding to his distress.'

'I'd far rather he were distressed than dead!' said I.

Holmes stopped in his tracks. 'You have a way of cutting to the heart of a problem which is most refreshing,' said he. 'You are right, as always ... if matters are as I suspect, then Gregson may indeed still be in some danger. Never fear, friend Watson, I think I see a way out of the difficulty.'

He said no more, but continued on his way towards the shrubbery at the far end of the lawn, where Welsh was pottering about in an aimless fashion, seemingly there because it was expected, rather than for any serious purpose. As we approached, the gardener straightened his back and smiled as cheerfully as he could.

'Gentlemen, good morning.'

'This is Mr Sherlock Holmes,' I told him. 'The local police have asked him to look into this dreadful business of Mr Morgan's death.'

'Of course, we've heard of you even down here, Mr Holmes. I'm only sorry it had to be this which brought you here, sir.'

'I understand that you were inside when the murder took place?'

Welsh's face clouded. 'I must have been, sir. And I have to confess that I did not sleep very well last night because of that ... if I had taken my tea outside, as I generally do, then I might have seen whoever it was, stopped them, even.'

'Come now, Welsh,' I told him, 'you can hardly blame yourself!'

'I do, though, sir, and that's a fact.'

'Could you tell us about the events of the afternoon?' said Holmes. 'Or is it inconvenient ... time for your luncheon, perhaps?'

Welsh took a handsome gold watch from his waistcoat pocket, and studied it. 'Half an hour to go, sir. I eat when the gentlemen do, you see ... saves the wife doing two lots of everything. Not that I can tell you much that you won't already know,' he added.

'Be that as it may, you might just supply a missing piece of the puzzle,' Holmes told him.

'Very well, sir. Shall we sit down?' and Welsh led the way to a sort of rustic arbour, complete with a bench.

Holmes handed him a cigar.

'Thank you, sir. But if it's all the same to you, I'll keep it for after my dinner ... it wouldn't do for the secretary to see me smoking during the day, especially not with the gentlemen, as it were.'

'I quite understand. Now, about yesterday? You were, I believe, working out here just before three o'clock?'

'I was, sir. Me and young John ... John Merryweather.'
Holmes glanced round the garden. 'He is not here today?'
'Sent word he wasn't feeling well, sir. I can believe that,' said
Welsh with a wry smile, 'for he was upset enough in all
conscience yesterday ... sick as a dog, if you'll excuse the
expression. Mind you, I wasn't exactly delighted myself.
Turned me over, it did.'

'But you are an old soldier, surely?'

'Dr Watson tell you that, did he, sir? Yes, it's true enough
that I did my time, and saw many a dead 'un ... killed a few
myself, too, come to that. But that was in the heat of battle, as
you might say. When it happens on your very doorstep, so to
speak, it's a different matter.'

'It must indeed have been a considerable shock.'

Welsh nodded without speaking.

'You went inside for a cup of tea at three o'clock?' prompted
Holmes.

'On the dot, sir. It's the only way here. You see, although
there are never more than six or seven gentlemen staying in the
house, by the same token there's only the wife and a couple of
maids ... and the maids are just women from the village, who
come in by the day. The wife does what she can to keep them
up to the mark, but there's still a lot to do, and too few pairs of
hands. So, three o'clock each day, I have my tea ... and so does
the wife, she has what you might call a bit of a breather before
putting the kettle back on for the gentlemen's tea at four.'

'And you drank your tea in the kitchen. Was that your
normal practice?'

Welsh's face clouded. 'It wasn't, sir. That's what bothers me
... in the usual way of things, it being summer, I'd have brought
my tea out here. That's what I do, as a rule, this hot weather.
Winter, now, I find jobs to do round the house ... an old place
like this takes some keeping up to, of course ... or if by some
chance I've had to be outside, well, it's pleasant to have ten
minutes warm by the stove.' He stared out over the lawn. 'I still
keep thinking that if I'd come outside, I might have done
something, sir.'

'If it's any consolation ...' I began.

Holmes cut me short. 'Was there some particular reason that you stayed inside yesterday?'

Welsh seemed to consider this for a time. 'Not what you would call particular, sir.' He hesitated.

'Come, now, Welsh,' said Holmes sternly, 'you must understand that in a case of murder, anything that is at all out of the ordinary must be questioned.'

'Yes, sir,' said Welsh, glumly. 'But I can take my oath that it had no bearing on Mr Morgan being killed.'

'Let us be the judge of that,' said Holmes.

'You'll both be married, gentlemen?'

Holmes looked nonplussed at the question.

'I am a widower,' said I.

'Then you'll know, Doctor, that a husband and wife don't always exactly see eye to eye,' said Welsh. 'It's this way … this job doesn't pay very much, but we do get our board and lodging, so our bit of money is ours. We've never been ones for throwing money about … I like my pipe, and a new suit every couple of years, and I treated myself to a decent watch a couple of years back, as you see, but I don't spend every evening in the pub as some do. Similarly, the wife likes a new hat now and then, which of them doesn't? But still we put a goodish bit in the Savings Bank each week, and over the years we've built up a modest little nest-egg. Now, we've talked about a pub of our own, or a little tobacconist's in the town, though I fancy a little market garden, being as gardening is my hobby as well as my profession, as you might say. There was no argument there, only a friendly discussion as to just what we would do. But the difference between us was just this … the wife's mother.'

'Ah!' said I, with a sudden access of understanding.

'The old lady lives in London, you see,' said Welsh, getting fairly into his stride, 'and she's happy enough there, with her old cronies. She doesn't want to live in the country … doesn't like it. But I can't live in London, couldn't do it if you paid me. That was all about it, gentlemen.'

'You had words over your mother-in-law, then?' said Holmes.

'Not words, sir, not words as such. Just wondering what to do for the best, talking it over, as it were. But then, blow me if I don't say something or the other about the old lady ... and I couldn't tell you just what it was I did say ... and the wife takes it entirely the wrong way! She flounces out of the kitchen and into our little parlour, leaving me holding my cup of tea with egg on my face, as you might say. Now, what was I to do? If I came out here, she'd be sure to accuse me of ignoring her, while if I followed her, she'd be sure to say I was picking a quarrel! So, I'm standing there, feeling like ... well, I won't say what ... when I hear someone shouting and carrying on in the dining room. Then there's a knocking at the door, the door between the kitchen and dining room, you know, sir.'

'And you very naturally went in to investigate?'

'At first, I thought one of the gentlemen must have been taken bad, or had an accident. Some of the older gentlemen, you understand, have had funny turns, or slipped on the stairs, things like that. So, I went in, through the door from the kitchen to the dining room, expecting the worst, you might say. But I wasn't exactly prepared for what had happened.'

'What did you do?'

'I couldn't say, sir, not exactly. Everything happened at once, you might say. I shoved Mr Gregson out of the way ... he seemed taken very bad, sir, hysterical like, a bit like the wife's sister was once took ... and I looked to see if Mr Morgan was dead, or just hurt.'

'Not much doubt?' I said.

'No, Doctor. I've seen a few in my time, but even if you hadn't, you couldn't think he was anything but a goner. Then a couple of the gentlemen came in ... Mr Tomlinson and Mr Pountney, it was ... and they sort of took over. Mr Pountney got Mr Gregson out of it ... he was still carrying on fit to burst ... and Mr Tomlinson, he went to fetch the secretary.'

'While you stayed in the dining room?'

Welsh nodded. 'I stepped over poor Mr Morgan, sir, being careful not to disturb anything ... we may be out of the way here, but I know how these things should be handled ... and checked the outside door. It was closed, but it wasn't locked, and I thought maybe ... you know? So, I called over to John, who was sitting out in the garden with his tea, had he seen anyone go that way? He looks at me, not really knowing what I'm on about, then he looks round and says, no. And then he realizes something is not quite right, and he comes over and sees Mr Morgan. And then he had to take himself off into the shrubbery. A small place like this, I expect it was the first body he's seen ... the first to die like that, at any rate. You know what it's like ... these youngsters have to pretend that they know it all, nothing shocks them, and all the time they don't know their aspidistra from their elbow, so to speak.'

'Indeed not,' said Holmes. 'Your first thought, then, was that the murderer had approached through the garden, and the outer door?'

Welsh hesitated once again. 'Not exactly my first thought, sir, no,' he mumbled.

'Come now, Welsh!'

'The truth is, I don't know just what I did think when I first got in there. Bewildered, you might say ... after all, Mr Holmes, what would you have thought? Mr Morgan lying there, dead as mutton, and Mr Gregson more or less standing over him? I ask you, what would you think, sir?'

'It must have been confusing,' agreed Holmes.

'It was, sir. Then I bethought myself, no, he'd not draw attention to himself like that, had he done it, now would he? And I didn't see how anyone could have got in through the house ... oh, it gets quiet, sometimes, when all the gentlemen are out, but even so, there's usually someone around. I knew that Fred Evans had been working round the front, he'd have seen any strangers. I nips out and I asks Fred, and he says, no there's been nobody out there all afternoon.'

'You were certain it must be a stranger, then?'

'I hardly like to think of it being one of the gentlemen, sir!'

'Of course not,' said Holmes. 'Tell me, did this Evans not come round to the kitchen for a cup of tea?'

Welsh grinned. 'He's not much of a one for tea, isn't Fred,' said he. 'More in the way of calling in at the pub on the way home.'

'I see. And then presumably Mr Morrison came along and summoned the police, and so forth?'

'That's right, sir. I kept out of the way after that, apart from helping to take poor Mr Morgan into the library when they asked me to.'

'Well,' said Holmes, 'that is all very clear, and very helpful. It is something of a pity that this assistant of yours ... John Merryweather, is it? ... is not here. I would have wished for a word with him, not that I expect his evidence to differ appreciably from yours.'

'He should be here tomorrow, sir. Of course, if you really wanted to see him, he lives just half a mile down the lane, with his father. A big house, it is, "Cherry Trees". A sign on the gate and all.'

'His father is a gardener, as well, I take it, then?'

Welsh grinned. 'Bless you, no, sir. His father has a name for being one of the richest men in these parts, though he doesn't get out much these days.'

'Oh?' Holmes looked puzzled.

'It's this way, sir ... the lad ... or I ought to say, the young gentleman ... plans to study for an estate manager, or something of the sort. He came to us before going up to the university, to get his hand in, as you might say. He's just here for a month or two, before he starts his studies in earnest.'

'Oh, I see. And this house, "Cherry Trees", you say? Down the lane?'

'Down the lane towards the village and turn left, sir.'

Holmes thanked him, and Welsh gave his curious little salute, studied his watch again, and made his way slowly towards the kitchen. Holmes pulled out his watch, and said, 'It is almost the hour of luncheon, Watson. Shall we join the others, or shall we go see this lad, while Welsh's testimony is still fresh in our memories?'

'I ate a decent breakfast,' I told him, 'and can happily last until dinner ... though not too much longer. But you have been travelling ... are you not hungry?'

'Not I. Not when I am fairly on the scent.'

'And you believe we are on the scent, Holmes? The whole business merely seems darker by the minute to me.'

Holmes led the way round to the front of the house and into the lane. 'But we are building up some sort of picture, slowly but surely,' he told me. 'What think you to Welsh's tale?'

'In what way? Did it not ring true to you?'

'It did. But that does not mean it was true.'

'But, Holmes! The fellow is so transparently honest! Salt of the earth!'

'An excellent fellow, indeed. And yet he quarrels with his wife.'

'I would hardly label it a quarrel. A minor difference of opinion, no more. Had you ever married, Holmes, you would be only too well aware how easily these things arise ... and how very often!'

Holmes laughed. 'I bow to your greater knowledge,' said he, then he nodded down the lane, where an elderly man was moving slowly ahead of us. 'I will wager that this is the third gardener,' said Holmes in a low voice. He increased his stride, and in a moment we had caught up with the old man. 'Mr Frederick Evans, I think?' said Holmes.

The old man looked at us suspiciously. 'Maybe. And who might you be?'

'My name is Sherlock Holmes, and this is my friend and associate, Dr Watson.' Holmes paused, confident that this announcement would have its usual effect.

'Oh? I'm very happy for you, I'm sure.' And the old fellow made as if to turn away.

'Evans,' said I, 'we are staying at Belmont, and Mr Morrison has asked us to investigate yesterday's dreadful occurrence.'

'Oh, has he, sir? Beg pardon, I'm sure, Doctor. Yes, I'm Fred Evans.' He looked anxiously from one to the other of us. 'But I'm sure I don't know nothing about it, gents. Nothing. No.'

'You were working in the front garden, I believe?' asked Holmes.

'That I was, sir. All day.'

'You never left the garden?'

Evans hesitated.

'You did not take a little stroll, as you are doing now, for example?' Holmes prompted him.

Evans scratched his head, then indicated a rather mouldy old canvas knapsack affair which was slung over one shoulder. 'I usually brings me dinner, sir,' said he. 'What you gents'd call luncheon, I expect. A bit of bread and cheese, bacon if I can get it. Very tasty, and all, but ...'

'A bit dry, sometimes?' said Holmes.

'You have it, sir. I usually take a walk along the lane about one o'clock, have a quick half at the pub here.' He waved a grimy hand at a shabby and uninviting hostelry by the side of the road.

'Very understandable,' said Holmes. 'And that you did yesterday, as well?'

'Yes, sir. But the rest of the time, I never left the garden. The first I knew was when Ernest Welsh come to ask me if anyone had gone through the front garden, and I says, no, and he rushes back inside. Then the police came ... and still no beggar told me what was going on! And then Ernie he came out again later, tells me what's happened ... poor gent! ... and asks me to help him move the corpse. And then the police asked me, had I seen any strangers, and I said no again. I hadn't, you see.'

'You are certain you saw no-one who ought not to have been there?'

'It's a quiet old place, sir, as you'll have seen. Even quieter working outside on your own. You notice anything, welcome it as a break from the work, you might say.'

'And so, you would very naturally recall anyone you saw? Who did you see yesterday, if I may ask?'

'Postman came, sir, name of Henry Garrity, first thing. And again, getting on towards dinner time, luncheon, or what you call it, twelve o'clock time. Butcher's boy came, pretty early, and the grocer. That was all. Apart from the gentlemen, of course, they're back and forth all day.'

'I expect you don't take any particular notice of which of the gentlemen came and went, or just when?' asked Holmes.

'I don't, sir, and that's a fact. We don't exactly get introduced, as you might say,' said Evans with a grin. 'I

81

remember the big chap, the one with the beard, he went out pretty early.'

'Mr Davenport?' I said.

Evans shrugged. 'If that's his name, sir. As I say, I don't know 'em to speak to, but I recall him, for he gave me a cigar last week, and complimented me on keeping the garden tidy. Most of them don't even notice.'

'I was most impressed by your moss roses,' Holmes told him.

'Indeed, sir? They're my pride and joy, you might say. A bit dusty now, with this hot weather, but you should've been here last week, they were really lovely.'

'You had not seen anyone odd … tramps, gypsies, or the like … hanging about in the lane?' asked Holmes.

Evans shook his head. 'Nothing of that sort round here, sir. A very peaceful little spot.' His gaze shifted involuntarily to the inn.

'Well,' said Holmes, 'we must not keep you any longer from your luncheon.' He took a coin or two from his pocket. 'You will perhaps be good enough to drink my health, sir?'

Evans touched his grubby cap. 'That I will, sir.'

Holmes set off once more down the lane. 'Well, Watson?'

'Well, it seems clear that anyone at all could have approached the house unobserved at the hour of luncheon. This Evans had absented himself, to wet his whistle, the guests were at luncheon, as was Welsh, by his own account. And, for full measure, Mrs Welsh, the cook, and the maids would all have been busy serving the meal. Now, the dining room was full, so nobody could get in there through the porch, but absolutely anyone could have gone in by the front door.' I waved a hand at the leafy lane. 'It is a quiet spot indeed, Holmes.' I lifted my stick over my head, and made to club him with it. 'Why, I could murder you here, in broad daylight, and who would know?'

At that moment an errand boy cycled past, ringing his bell furiously as he passed us, although we were on the other side of the road. Holmes and I looked at one another, and burst out laughing.

'Well, you would have one witness against you, Watson!'

'But the general point is a good one?'

'H'mm. Good enough, perhaps. I do not dispute the quietness of the place. The problem is just this, Watson ... I do not give too much credence to the theory of an itinerant murderer. It is not a generally recognized profession.'

'Perhaps not, Holmes, but the profession of itinerant sneak-thief is well enough known!' said I with some heat. 'Suppose some tramp had indeed entered the house, stolen the letter opener ... and perhaps other items which have not yet been missed ... then come back downstairs just as Evans returned from the pub? The thief could not leave by the front door without Evans seeing him, and he could not go through the dining room, where luncheon was being served. What does he do, then? Why, he hides in the cloakroom by the front door. He hears the guests disperse after luncheon, but perhaps the maids, or Mrs Welsh, are moving about, dusting and so forth. He skulks there until all is quiet, at around three o'clock. He peeps out ... Gregson is smoking at the front door, so the thief sneaks into the dining room, makes his way to the porch ... he does not know Morgan is in there ... pulls open the inside door, and ... and there you are!'

'It certainly has much to recommend it as a theory,' said Holmes, 'but there are certain objections.'

'Why, so there are to any theory we have thus far formulated!'

'True enough.' Holmes pointed with his stick. 'This is our road, I fancy. Tell me, since we are theorizing, what say you to this ... Welsh did not quarrel with his wife over her mother, but because he believed she was involved with Gregson.'

'Holmes!'

'Is it so fanciful, then? Mrs Welsh is not unattractive, is she?'

'In a matronly sort of way, I suppose ...'

'And these are egalitarian times, Watson, a man may easily take a fancy to a housekeeper. Especially a man such as Gregson ... why, did not you yourself call him a mangy tom cat, or something of the kind?'

'Stuff and nonsense, Holmes! Anyway, it would be an easy enough matter to ask Mrs Welsh what they spoke about, surely?

'A wife cannot testify against her husband,' said Holmes in an abstracted fashion. 'Anyway, Mrs Welsh might not associate the quarrel with the murder, and if she did, she might well decide that it were best not to get her husband into trouble. No, let us continue ... suppose Welsh had some cause for jealousy ... or simply believed that he had such cause ... and had words with his wife? She leaves, angry. Welsh knows that Gregson is in the porch, for he has seen him go in from the garden. He does not know that Gregson has left, and Morgan gone in. Blind with jealousy, Welsh bursts into the dining room, pulls open the door of the porch, and ... with a practised hand, a hand used to wielding the bayonet ... he stabs at the man inside.'

'With a letter opener that is upstairs in Gregson's room?' I scoffed.

'That is one objection, but it is the one overwhelming objection that must needs be met whatever theory we adopt. Suppose that the jealous Welsh had taken the letter opener earlier, and was just waiting for the opportunity to use it? Is there not a poetic justice in killing a man with his own knife, after all?'

'It is a theory,' said I. 'But I don't believe it for one moment. Do you?'

'It is a theory,' Holmes agreed.

'Welsh is so obviously devoted to his wife! Incapable of dishonesty, or anger!'

'Perhaps. Ah, "Cherry Trees". Aptly named.' He waved his stick at the trees which had given the house its name, now devoid of all but a few lingering blossoms. 'A metaphor of life itself, Doctor. In full flower one moment, and then the next ... the harsh winds of reality reduce one to a pile of rubbish, fit only for burning! Ah, me!'

In no mood for introspection, I snorted and briskly led the way up a broad gravel path, and rang the doorbell vigorously. An elderly and respectable housekeeper opened it almost at once, and regarded me suspiciously.

'Might we see Mr John Merryweather?' said I. 'This is Mr Sherlock Holmes, and I am Doctor John Watson.'

'Oh, Doctor! Yes, indeed, sir. Come in, come in. And your friend,' she added, looking through Holmes.

The housekeeper led the way through the house without stopping, until we came to a door on the far side. She opened this, and took us out on to a kind of terrace, overlooking a large but somewhat untidy garden. A pale young man of twenty or so sat on the terrace in a wicker chair. As we approached, he got up and looked from one to another of us.

'This gentleman is a doctor, Mr John,' the housekeeper told him.

'Really, Mrs Timms!' His voice was a mixture of irritation and amusement. 'I fear Mrs Timms has been over-anxious, sir. Your services are really not required. But now you are here, may I offer you some refreshment?'

'It was not Mrs Timms who sent for us,' said Holmes. 'We are here in connection with the sad business at Belmont yesterday. I am Sherlock Holmes, and this is Doctor John Watson.'

'Oh, I see.' His face became grave. 'Will you sit down?' and he waved us to chairs. 'Mrs Timms, would you bring us some tea? Unless ...'

'Tea would be most acceptable,' said Holmes.

'You will excuse the misunderstanding,' said Merryweather, when the housekeeper had gone. 'Your names are familiar to me from the pages of the *Strand*, of course, and it comes as no surprise that the local police should have called upon your services. But when Mrs Timms said you were a doctor, sir, I naturally assumed at the outset that she had sent for you to take a look at me.'

'Are you unwell, then?' said I.

'Not in the least, sir! And I told Mrs Timms as much yesterday, and again this morning. Shaky, I allow. Upset. But then who would not be?'

'Indeed,' said Holmes. His perceptive glance took in the garden. 'You are, as I understand it, about to undertake a course of study in horticulture?'

'In estate management, sir. We ... the would-be students, I mean ... were told that it might be as well if we had some little practical experience before commencing the more theoretical portion of the course. Some of the chaps I know are at the Royal Botanic Gardens, some working on farms or the like. But I knew that an extra gardener was sought at Belmont, if one could be persuaded to come cheap, and it is but a few minutes' walk away, so what could be better? Although with my duties in the Belmont garden, I have rather neglected this one, I fear. Ah,' he went on, as the housekeeper returned with a tray, 'thank you, Mrs Timms. Help yourselves, gentlemen.'

'Thank you,' said Holmes, pouring tea for us all. He looked round the garden once more. 'This is your father's house, is it not?'

'It is, sir.' The youth's face clouded slightly. 'He is, I regret to say, not in the best of health himself.'

'Indeed?' said I. 'Despite any initial misunderstandings, I am in truth a medical man, so if I may be of any assistance ...'

'It is most kind of you, Dr Watson, but he has had good advice. The truth is, he is not so much physically ill as disturbed in his mind ... oh,' he added quickly, 'nothing unpleasant, you understand. He is, as I might say, something of a recluse, that is all. He has been for some time, now, since the loss of my mother. That is why I decided to turn an interest in horticulture and agriculture into what will, I hope, be a lucrative career. That, and a certain reluctance to become too much of a recluse in my turn. We ... Mrs Timms, myself, the maids ... we try to keep anything troublesome from intruding upon him. In fact, I have not yet told him any details of what occurred yesterday. I did say that there had been an accident ... I feared lest the maids, for all their care, might let something out about it, and thought it as well to prepare him.'

'I understand perfectly,' said Holmes. 'Now, I know this may be distressing to you, but I should like to ask about the events of yesterday.'

'Of course, but I can really tell you nothing I have not already told the police.'

'You went into the house at three o'clock?'

Merryweather nodded. 'I had had something of an upset stomach all day ... the collywobbles, as old Mrs Timms is wont to call them ... and used the domestic offices next to the kitchen. I went into the kitchen itself, washed my hands at the sink, and took my tea outside.'

'You would normally use the outside offices?'

Merryweather gave a strained smile. 'It is that, or go right through the kitchen to the offices used by the maids. The outside place is quite adequate.'

'You would not go into the main house for that purpose, then?'

'Lord, no!' Merryweather looked shocked. 'Not at all the done thing! I must confess, I had not hitherto thought about the invisible barriers ... the kitchen door, beyond which the outside staff pass only by permission of the housekeeper; and ... more to the point ... the baize door between the masters and servants. I trust that my few weeks at Belmont have made me more considerate of our own poor little Abigails ... and dear Mrs Timms ... though I fear the effect will be only temporary.'

'It may have a more profound effect,' said Holmes. 'The spirit, the animus or persona of the ancients, is a strange and wonderful thing indeed. And how long was it between your leaving the garden to come inside, and your returning with your tea?'

'Oh ... five minutes? About that.'

'It could not have been ten?'

'I cannot swear that it was not. Between five and ten minutes, not much less, but certainly not more.'

'Very well. Were Welsh and his wife in the kitchen when you went to wash?'

'Yes, sir. They seemed ... well, they seemed to be having some sort of discussion ... not a heated argument by any means, but a mild difference of opinion, perhaps. The atmosphere seemed a touch strained when I went in, so I did not stay, as I might otherwise have done, but took my tea outside.'

'And then?'

87

'And then the next thing I knew, Welsh opened the door of the porch thing, and shouted across to me. I could not make him out at first, and then I realized that he was asking was there any intruder in the garden.'

'And was there?'

'No, no-one. I said as much, then ... being naturally curious as to what was going on ... I went across to the house, and saw ...' and he broke off, his face turning paler yet.

'Do not distress yourself,' said Holmes in his most soothing tones.

'No, I'm all right. I was not, then, I confess ... my upset stomach showed its displeasure, and with a vengeance. I hung around until the police had questioned me ... I told them just what I've told you now ... and then slunk back here, and passed a most unpleasant night.'

'And you are quite certain there could have been nobody in the garden?'

'As certain as I can be. Mr Welsh and I were working up by the house, so there might have been someone lurking further down, where it is more overgrown, but I think not. There are rooks in the old trees at the far end, and they reveal the presence of any intruders.'

'And they did not do so yesterday?'

'No, sir. I think Mr Welsh and I would have known had there been anyone there ... it is a quiet place, and we should have heard the birds, as I say, or seen some other sign.'

'But you could not swear as to what might have been going on whilst you were in the house.'

'Well ... I suppose not. But I can tell you that if anyone did come to the house and leave again by the garden, then he must have been a pretty useful sprinter.'

Holmes laughed, and got up. 'Thank you for the tea. By the way, there is a lane of sorts at the back of Belmont, is there not?'

'Yes. You go a little further down the road in front of this house, take the first right, then right again. It is more a wide footpath than a real lane, but it takes you back to Belmont. There is a gate and a stile, and a rustic notice board telling trespassers to keep out.'

'Thank you,' said Holmes.

'And may I express the hope that your father's health may improve?' I added.

'It is very good of you, sir, but I fear that the best I can hope for is that it will get no worse.'

'Then by all means let us hope for that,' said Holmes, shaking the young man's hand. 'And now we must leave you.'

Six

'And what do you think to that young man, Watson?' asked Holmes as he set off down the road.

'He seems forthright enough. And his testimony corroborates what we already knew.'

'Indeed. One thing emerged, and that is that the outside staff were not in the habit if venturing into the main house, although Welsh is obviously an exception. The letter opener, then, must have been taken from Gregson's room either by a guest, or by one of the inside servants.'

'You entirely dismiss the notion of a tramp, or casual burglar, then?'

'I put it low on the list of possibilities, let us say. The guests are perhaps the most likely candidates, although I agree that it is not a pleasant thought.' He frowned. 'Or the Welshes? H'mm.'

'Perhaps one of the maids ...'

'They are "maids" by courtesy only, I fear,' said Holmes. 'Both are, you will have observed, rather elderly and respectable women. Neither struck me as having a homicidal gleam in her eye, or ... though it is perhaps a trifle ungallant to say it ... as being likely to have a lover to whom the letter opener might be handed for use as a weapon.'

'And by the same token, and despite your plausible arguments, I am inclined to dismiss the Welshes, husband and wife,' said I. 'Apart from their patent honesty, neither of them appears to me to have any good reason to kill one of the guests. Which does just leave one of the guests, unpalatable though the idea undoubtedly is, just as you say.' I stopped dead in my tracks, and looked him squarely in the eye. 'Holmes, I am growing increasingly concerned about Gregson ... do you really think we are justified in letting him go on all unknowing and unsuspicious?'

Holmes pointed with his stick. 'This is our lane, Watson. Yes, you are right. I shall take steps to ensure that Gregson has nothing to fear from the killer, always assuming that Gregson was the intended victim.'

I started down the lane he had indicated. 'I am glad to hear you say so, Holmes. This must be the footpath the lad spoke of,' I added, leading the way off to the right.

A walk of under half a mile along a path, dark and cool in the shade of the great trees on either hand, brought us to a gate, with a roughly made notice board reading, 'Belmont. Private. Keep out.' I made as if to enter, but Holmes pulled me back.

'A moment, Watson. I am anxious to examine the outside of the house, and the garden, but they will still be at luncheon, and I do not want to disturb them.'

'Or let them see what you are up to, Holmes?'

'As you say. So, let us first take this opportunity to look at this end of the garden, for your tramps or gypsies must needs have come this way.' He examined the gate thoroughly. 'Nothing to be made of that, I fear. Recently oiled, by Welsh, I suppose.' He opened the gate, and set off up a steep and narrow path, all overgrown with weeds. 'Someone has passed this way, you see,' he said, pointing to where some of the weeds and brambles had been roughly pushed aside. 'That may be Welsh again, of course, or any of the guests who have a taste for solitary rambling.'

'I came this way myself, yesterday morning,' said I.

'It is probably used all the time,' said Holmes, with some chagrin in his voice. He set off through the gate without more ado.

The path led up through tall old trees, which did an excellent job of concealing us from anyone looking out of the house, or the more formal section of the garden. But those old trees held the rookery of which Merryweather had spoken, and as Holmes moved ahead of me, the birds cawed and fluttered, expressing their displeasure at the disturbance of their afternoon's rest.

'Excellent sentinels, Holmes!' said I.

'Indeed, Watson,' he replied, with just a touch of disapproval, for he had an odd trait of refusing to accept anything he had been told without verifying it for himself. 'We may assume that the gardeners would have been alerted to any outsider coming this way.' He diverted from the path. 'H'mm. The same would apply to anyone climbing over the wall.'

'They might have come over the fence from next door,' I suggested, pointing to the boundary.

'Yes, but they must still conceal themselves here, or hereabouts, and that would alert the rooks. I think we may rule this approach out.' He left the trees, and stood on the edge of the lawn which led up to the house. 'Right, Watson. You are concealed here, having somehow managed not to alert the rooks. You see the gardeners go inside, and you set off. Could you reach the house, stab your victim, and return in five minutes?'

'Easily! But I would not care to. Why, if anyone looked out of any of those windows, they could not miss you!'

'Of course, they could not fail to miss you. Now ... but what's this?' and he broke off as Welsh, his face grim, came through the trees towards us.

'Now, then ... oh, it's you gents!' Welsh's face cleared. 'Sorry, gentlemen, I thought it might have been ... you know? I heard the old birds cawing, and thought that someone was down here who shouldn't be.'

'I wanted to see if we could approach the house from the back lane without being seen,' said Holmes.

Welsh shook his head. 'Can't be done, begging your pardon, sir. Anyone in the garden must be certain to hear those birds. Wasn't it the old Greeks, or Romans, or someone kept geese, for the same reason? Well, geese let you know if anyone comes calling all right, but I'd back the rooks any day.'

'I think you are right,' said Holmes. 'Is luncheon over?'

'Mine is, sir,' said Welsh, grinning broadly. 'The gentlemen might still be at table, of course.'

'No matter,' said Holmes. 'I want a look at the outside of the house,' and he suited his actions to his words, strolling up and down the lawn, examining the house from every angle. Welsh looked at Holmes for a while, then went off to his work.

'Well, Holmes?' said I at the end of ten minutes.

'As we have shown, it would be both difficult and dangerous to approach from this end of the garden, right enough,' said he. 'But consider this, Watson ... someone in the library, looking out of the window, would see gardeners and Gregson alike enter the house. There is not a French window as such in the library, but the windows in there come close ... you observe that they are quite large enough for a man to get through, and the sills are no more than two feet from the ground. Our man might easily climb out, take ... what? ... six or seven paces to the porch, commit the crime, and hasten back.'

'But Lane was in the library!'

'Asleep, by his own account.'

'The unknown assailant must have moved quietly, so as not to wake him? I do not believe it could be done! And again, it is less a question of whether it could be done, as of whether anyone would dare to do it, and risk detection.'

'The objection disappears if it were Lane himself who did it,' said Holmes.

'And what reason would he have?'

'Lane himself suggested that he was Morgan's long-lost nephew. He spoke in jest ... or what he considered a jest ... but he might easily have had some prior connection with either Gregson or Morgan. As Lane himself said, we do not know just what the relations between the various guests may or may not have been.'

'It is certainly a possibility,' said I. 'And yet another is that a man in the sitting room would similarly see what went on in the garden. It is a slightly longer walk from there, but not by much ... far less dangerous than going across the lawn.'

94

'True enough, and Tomlinson was in the sitting room, was he not?'

'So Lane said. But I must point out ... although it was my own suggestion ... that if anyone went from the sitting room, he must pass the library.'

'The sole occupant of which was asleep!'

'He would not know that in advance,' I pointed out.

'True,' said Holmes, 'but it was no very great danger. It was a hot day, what were the chances of anyone being inside the library? He might legitimately think that they were all outside, enjoying the fresh air. And if anyone did see him, he could simply wave a greeting, make some remark about how hot the day was, or so on. All innocent enough.'

'He would not be able to go through with his plan, though. He would only seem to be innocently enjoying a stroll in the grounds as long as no murder were discovered.'

'He would not be able to go through with his plan,' repeated Holmes thoughtfully. 'That is quite true, but then he might have another opportunity later. He may well have thought that it was worth a try, worth the small risk involved.'

'Granted. In either instance, the thing could easily be called off were he seen going to the porch. The real danger would be on the return trip, assuming the murder were carried out successfully ... successfully from the murderer's viewpoint, that is,' said I.

'You sum it up in your usual perceptive manner,' said Holmes. 'The real danger was indeed that he might be seen on the return trip.'

'It must have been desperation indeed to cause him to run such a risk.'

'Or suddenly seeing the opportunity, perhaps?' said Holmes. He waved a hand at the first-floor windows. 'Much the same argument applies to anyone looking out from one of the bedrooms,' he went on. 'In that instance, we must postulate their going downstairs and through the dining room. Again, some danger of detection, but surely not much? The gardeners were inside, as far as our man knew, at any rate, and he could not know that there had been some slight activity, comings and goings in the telephone cubicle.'

'And if he were upstairs, that might account for Gregson's letter opener … the murderer might have taken that on his way down, for, having seen Gregson enter the porch, the murderer would know that he could not be in his room!'

'Well done, Watson! Pountney was upstairs, was he not?'

'So I gather. And someone mentioned that Morrison had also to be brought from his room.'

'Indeed. We must talk to them, I think.'

'But first you had promised to do something about Gregson, and the possible danger he may still be in.'

'H'mm.' Holmes cautiously approached the outside door of the porch, but before he could touch the handle, the door swung open, and Gregson himself appeared.

'Oh!' Gregson stood to one side. 'Were you wanting to use the telephone?'

'If luncheon is quite finished,' said Holmes. 'But am I interrupting you?'

'No, no. I have just spoken to … well, to Sarah, the gallery owner. I just wanted to confirm that everything has been satisfactorily resolved.'

'And has it?'

'Oh, yes.' Gregson hesitated. 'It might seem a touch … unfeeling, perhaps? To be concerned about relatively minor details, with poor Morgan lying in his coffin.' He shrugged his shoulders, as if to shake off any possible criticism. 'It would have worried me, though, had I not cleared the matter up, and, after all, it cannot hurt Ben now. Well, sir, I shall leave you to it,' and he set off down the garden.

'I shall not keep you a moment, Doctor,' said Holmes, and he went into the little porch and closed the door after him.

I stared at the garden, and then at the outside of the old house, trying to imagine what had occurred yesterday. Without success, I may add, for it all seemed most dark and puzzling to me. I heard the porch door open, and set off towards it, thinking that Holmes had finished his telephone call. He had not quite done, though, and I caught his last few words – 'No, no! After dinner will be soon enough, I fancy! Goodbye!' He replaced the instrument, and rejoined me. 'That should do it, I think, Watson. And now, let us resume our investigations.'

Before I could ask what he had arranged, he led the way along the side of the house to the french windows in the sitting room, and went inside. The only occupant was Morrison, who sat disconsolate in an armchair. He looked up as we went in, and said, 'Hullo! Discovered anything yet?'

'Nothing of any significance,' said Holmes. 'But we are, I trust, building up a picture of what may have happened.'

'Are you, though? So, we may look for a speedy resolution of the matter?'

'I am hopeful that we may.'

'I shall be very glad of it,' said Morrison frankly, 'for I may say that the trustees are far from happy about it. At least, the chairman is, and I am sure that the others will not differ markedly in their views.'

'You have spoken to your chairman, then?'

Morrison nodded. 'He is a solicitor with an office in the village. I went along there this morning ... I dare not let him hear the news first from someone else, and he would have been certain to do so.'

'Well, I cannot honestly see that he can lay any blame at your door,' said Holmes.

'He takes the view ... very properly ... that I am in charge of the place, and thus responsible for what goes on here. Perhaps he is just a touch more rigid than he need be, but I have to abide by his decision. I tell you honestly, Mr Holmes, that if matters are not put right very soon, they will be looking for my resignation.' And he sunk into a deeper gloom.

'Have you held this post for long?' asked Holmes.

'Some three or four years.'

'And before that?'

'I worked in the City, a firm of shipping agents. It was more lucrative than this post, but far from congenial ... I enjoy the countryside, and I am, moreover, a lazy devil ... so when I heard of this post being vacant, I applied at once, and was lucky enough to secure it. The work is not arduous, the company has always been agreeable, and the life generally first-class. Until now, of course.'

'Of course. I understand you did not usually attend your office on a Tuesday?'

'No. The work, as I say, is not heavy, far from it. I can usually keep things running smoothly by looking in twice a week, Monday and Friday. But I had intended to take a couple of weeks off, and wanted to tidy up as many loose ends as possible. And now it is I who am at a loose end myself! Despite yesterday's alarums and excursions, I cleared up the very few outstanding bits of business, and so I do not really know what to do. The holiday must be cancelled, naturally, but I feel perfectly useless here.' He sighed. 'I may not stay here after tonight ... my cottage is quite close, so I can easily be reached if needs be, and I shall at least be able to potter in my own garden. In fact, I should have gone home this afternoon, were it not that it might smack of deserting my post.'

'I hardly think that you need view it in that light,' said Holmes with a smile.

'No, but I assure you that the chairman of the trustees would! On balance, I think I might go home now for an hour or so, reassure my wife and kiss my children, then return and spend the night here. Just in case.'

'If I might just put one or two questions to you before you leave?' asked Holmes.

'Of course.'

'You have, you say, been secretary here for only some three or four years. Did you know Morgan before you came here?'

Morrison shook his head. 'I had never heard of the place, until I was told that the secretary's post was vacant. The chap who told me was a regular guest here, but he is not staying here just at the moment. The ones who are here just now ... no, I met all of them only within the last three or four years. Since I took the post, in fact.'

'I see. Now, the outer door of the porch, where the telephone is situated. Is that usually locked, or not?'

'Welsh makes a point of checking that it is locked last thing at night, of course, when he does his rounds. However, he does not unlock it in a morning, in the same way that he unlocks the front door. If a guest lets himself out that way into the garden, then the door remains unlocked, for the key is on the inside, as perhaps you noticed. Again, if a guest comes in that way, he may well turn the key and lock the door after him.'

Holmes sighed wearily.

'It is, I fear, somewhat of an informal arrangement,' said Morrison, 'but it has served us well enough until now. We like the guests to feel that this is their home, for the time being, and so we have as few rules and regulations as possible. If each guest had a separate key to that door, of course, then we might insist that it remain locked unless in actual use, but, as it is, it is not truly a door as such, merely a convenient short-cut of sorts. The guests ought to use the front door, by rights, but then they would be obliged to walk right round the house to reach the garden, so we make no difficulty if they use the French windows in the sitting room, or the outer door of the porch.'

'So, the door might have been locked when Gregson first used the telephone? He would then unlock it to let himself out?'

'That may well have been the case,' said Morrison. 'Naturally, I cannot say whether it was, or no. You could ask Gregson?'

'That particular point is not important,' said Holmes. 'Now, Gregson used the outer door to go out to the garden, so he must have left the door unlocked.'

'He could not have locked it,' Morrison pointed out. 'There is just the one key for the use of guests, and that is left on the inside. I have a key, of course, and so does Welsh, but the guests do not. In order to lock the door from the outside, a guest would have to take the key out with him and retain it in his possession, and ... tolerant though we may be ... I would take a dim view of that.'

'Indeed. That is most clear. But, now, suppose a guest were to enter the house from the garden ... would he lock the door after him?'

'He might. I would,' said Morrison. 'In fact, I very often do. If there is nobody outside, and I come in by the porch door, I would usually lock it after me. As I say, we are fairly informal, but I believe in being as careful as may be.'

'Very wise. And the other guests?'

'Those who have been here before perhaps would, they know my little ways. But there is no hard and fast rule.'

'And, supposing you had entered and locked the door after you, what of someone coming to that door after you had locked it?'

'They could not get in that way, of course. And the French window in the dining room is usually locked, until dinner at least, when it might be opened if it were a warm evening. But the kitchen door is just round the side of the house here, and Mrs Welsh would make no difficulty about allowing you through there. But most guests would never think to go to the kitchen, they would simply walk along to the sitting room ... the French window there is usually unlocked, and there is a handle on the outside. If that window were, by some chance, locked as well, they would have to go to the front door.'

'And if that were locked to boot?' said I.

Morrison laughed. 'Well, they could always ring the bell!'

I laughed with him. 'Never thought of that!'

'We have at least a very comprehensive picture of the doors!' said Holmes. 'One or two other small points trouble me slightly. I gather that Gregson was in something of an hysterical state when he found the body?'

'Yes. "Proper took", as my old nurse used to put it.'

'Yes. Welsh was disturbed by the fuss, and so were Tomlinson, in the sitting room, which is at the other end of the house, and Pountney ... who was upstairs.'

'I fear you have lost me, Mr Holmes. Peter was, as you say, making a considerable racket, so why should they not be alarmed?'

'Why not, indeed?' Holmes paused, then, almost casually, added, 'How came you not to hear it, then? For I gather Tomlinson or one of the others had to summon you from your room?'

'Oh, I see! The secretary's office is little more than a box-room, Mr Holmes, as you saw. Tucked away right at the end of the upstairs corridor. And I had my door closed, for I do not care to be disturbed when I am working. Moreover, I have a typewriter for official correspondence, and the noise of that, and concentrating on hitting the right keys ... I suppose that all those things together had some effect. Then, Pountney's room is right at the head of the stairs, so that would account for his hearing anything in the dining room, whilst I could not. And Tomlinson ... well, he was down here, not upstairs.'

'Yes, I see. And when you realized that Morgan was dead, you summoned Inspector Forrester?'

'Immediately.'

'Did you send Welsh for him, or ...'

'No, I telephoned the local station ... I knew they have the telephone, of course.'

'What, you used the instrument in the porch?'

'No, no! I have another telephone in my room.'

Holmes sat up, alert. 'Is it connected with the telephone downstairs in the porch?'

Morrison shook his head. 'It is a quite separate line, with a different number at the exchange. You can see the two wires if you stand outside the house and look at the roof. The one downstairs is a sort of general one, mine is exclusively for the use of the secretary.'

'That was all I wished to know, thank you. Oh,' Holmes added, as Morrison got to his feet, 'are the other guests about the place, do you know?'

'I think Davenport is next door, in the library.'

'Thank you.'

Morrison nodded a last farewell, and made his way out into the corridor.

'We have indeed a comprehensive picture of the doors,' said I. 'But what exactly does it tell us?'

'It tells us that Gregson might well have locked the outer door when he went in.'

'We could always ask him! Anyway, we know he did not, for the door was open when the body was discovered.'

'The murderer might have unlocked it,' said Holmes. 'But that is not the significant point. Any guest who had been here before would know that there was at least a possibility of Gregson's locking that door after him.'

'And that would tend to preclude an approach from outside? Of course! You cannot very well kill someone through a locked door.'

'Well, there would be difficulties, would there not? The point is not whether the door was locked or not ... which is why I shall not bother to ask Gregson if he locked it ... but whether the murderer believed that it might be locked. It is another interesting point.'

'And the point about Morrison's telephone line?'

'Well, if it were an extension, and connected with the telephone downstairs, he might have been able to tell if the instrument were in use.'

'He would hardly listen to a private conversation, Holmes! And if he did, he would never admit it!'

'I did not think that of him. No, I thought merely that there might be a bell upstairs, or something of the kind, which would have told him that the downstairs instrument had been picked up or put down. As it is a separate line, then of course that is not the case, and so it cannot be a factor.'

Holmes got to his feet, and set off down the corridor. I followed as far as the door of the library, which Holmes opened. 'Hullo!' said he, to an occupant hidden from my view. There was a kind of mumbled greeting in response, and Holmes held the door open for me. I entered, to see James Davenport sitting morosely looking out of the window.

Holmes followed me in. 'We are not disturbing you?' he asked.

'Lord, no. I should be glad of someone to talk to, for this business is preying on my mind.' Davenport waved a large hand in a vague way at the chairs, and Holmes and I sat down.

'It is a distressing business, is it not?' said Holmes in his most soothing tones.

'That is putting it very politely, Mr Holmes! I called it "damnable" yesterday, and I have seen no good reason to amend that opinion.'

'You know me, then?' asked Holmes.

'I assumed you must be Mr Sherlock Holmes ... there has been some talk among the guests, as you will imagine. I confess, Dr Watson, that I had not immediately associated you with the Dr Watson of *Strand* fame.'

'You will know, then, that I am here at the request of the local police, and of Mr Morrison,' said Holmes. 'Would you have any objection to my asking you a few questions?'

'Heavens, no! But I must warn you that I can tell you nothing about Ben's sad death. I was not even in the house.'

'And where were you?'

Davenport waved a hand in the general direction of the window. 'Out there, somewhere. On the Downs, taking the air.'

'Alone?'

'I fear that I was. And by the same token, I fear that I did not stop at any wayside hostelry and invite the assembled throng to drink my health, nor did I dally with any buxom country wench who might later be relied upon to stand up in court and cry *Alibi!* in my defence.'

'That is a pity, in some respects,' said Holmes calmly. 'You returned ... when?'

'About half past three. I had proposed to have a wash ... which would have been most welcome ... before tea, which would have been doubly so. In the event, I had neither wash nor tea. I was aware that something was amiss as I came through the door. Welsh came out of the library, muttered something about Morgan. I could not quite make him out, and, at first, I thought it was an accident, or something of the kind. I went into the library, and found a little crowd in there ... Gregson, of course, Pountney, Tomlinson and Gordon Morrison.'

'Was Lane in there?'

Davenport shook his head.

'He had apparently been sleeping in the library earlier,' said Holmes.

'He certainly was not there when I went in. I did not see him until much later, mooching about with that damned notebook. Things were very confused, though, as you may imagine. Gregson was very upset, and I could not at first make out why, or what had happened. The police arrived very soon after I did, they took Gregson into the kitchen, I think, to speak privately to him, and it was only then that I got the chance to ask the others what the trouble was. I have seldom been so shocked in my life, and I could quite see why Gregson had been in such a state. The police questioned us all in our turn ... they did not waste too much time on me, I'm pleased to say, not when once I had told them that I had not been in the place. And then they cleared us out of the library, to take poor Morgan's body in for the surgeon to see him.'

'Thank you, that is very clear. Tell me, what reason would anyone have to kill Benjamin Morgan?'

Davenport shook his head. 'I'm damned if I can tell you. I always got on very well with him, and I think most of the others here did as well. Oh, there were odd differences of opinion, right enough ... when are there not? But nothing so bad as to murder for.'

'Had you known him long?'

'About ten years. We almost worked together once, that is how I came to meet him.'

'Almost?'

'Almost, but not quite.' Davenport stood up, surprisingly briskly for a man of his size, strode across to a shelf, and picked up a magazine the cover of which I recognized at once. 'The *Strand*, you see,' said Davenport. 'No wonder your fame precedes you, Mr Holmes! Now,' and he turned the magazine over to show the back cover, 'this is an example of the sort of work I do, producing plates for manufacturers wishing to advertise their wares, or illustrations for books on shells, or flowers, or the other diversions of the leisured classes. It is scarcely to be described as "Art" in any capital-letter sense, but it is a living. Oh, I produce my own creative engravings, prints which might reasonably have some pretensions to genuine artistic merit and originality, but I have never made any real money from those. It is, I fear, an old story.'

Holmes nodded.

'Rather like Pear's Soap and *Bubbles* do you mean?' I asked.

'Exactly, Doctor, save that in that instance the artist got full credit for his work. Well,' Davenport continued, 'some ten years ago, I was approached by an old-established firm of corn chandlers. They had an idea for a patent oatmeal, which would take the country by storm, turn our notions of breakfast on their heads. "The new oatmeal for the new century!" ... that was how they intended to sell it. And, being so new and up-to-date, they wanted no *Bubbles*, no mere painting, to advertise the new oatmeal. No, nothing would do but the new art of photography ... they proposed to take photographs of engaging little urchins actually eating the substance!'

'What was it called?' I asked.

'Oh, it never was put on the shelves. They tried it out on some of those same urchins, and they hated it. As I did ... dreadful stuff, tasted rather of rotten eggs.'

'Intriguing though these revelations are,' said Holmes sternly, 'I rather fear ...'

'I beg your pardon, Mr Holmes. Well, they had seen the success that *Bubbles* had been for the soap people, and they wanted to hire a famous photographer for their advertising pictures, include his name in the plate and so on. They asked me to contact Ben, who had already a considerable reputation as a portrait photographer.'

'And?'

'And he simply hit the roof! He was furious. He did not actually use the phrase "prostituting his art", or anything, but you could tell that was how he saw it. Ben had his own ideas, you see.'

'And what happened?'

'Nothing, really. Ben stuck to his principles and his portraits, I started work with another photographer, and then the corn merchants decided not to bother after all, and the whole enterprise fell through.'

'And you met Morgan again here?'

'He introduced me to the place. Indeed, we became firm friends, after he had initially blown me up as he did. We still differed about "Art", of course, he still rather looked down on me for my commercial work, though he seldom actually said as much.' Davenport laughed. 'It is strange, for then Gregson rather looked down on Ben in his turn, because Gregson does not consider photography to be an art form! You would see for yourselves if you spent any length of time here. There is almost a ... a hierarchy is not the right word ... but there are gradations, shades of opinion as to what is legitimate art and what is not. Very odd.'

'The artistic temperament?' I suggested.

'Just so, Doctor.'

'Did these ... gradations of belief ... ever cause open dissension here?' asked Holmes.

'Indeed, they did! We have had many a heated discussion on the topic.'

'And you took part in these ... discussions?'

'I started most of them,' said Davenport, with a smile. 'It seemed an excellent diversion to get Peter started on his hobby-horse and watch the fun. It probably seems pretty trivial, if not downright childish, to you, and I confess that it seems that way to me, now. But it did not always seem that way.'

'Were tempers ever lost during these discussions?'

Davenport hesitated.

'Come, sir!' said Holmes.

'Well, occasionally. Peter can be infuriating sometimes. It is odd ... he is an excellent sculptor, and very highly regarded by the critics and connoisseurs, and yet he feels constantly obliged to make himself look bigger by making others look smaller, if I make myself clear. He seems to have very little faith in his own talent and ability ... I have not the jargon to describe it properly, though some of the more advanced German mental specialists might have a word for it.'

'I am sure they would have,' said Holmes. 'But you say he infuriated you at times?'

'There were times when I could cheerfully have scragged him,' said Davenport. 'But ... just in case you were wondering ... that would have been in the heat of the moment, and in broad daylight to boot, not in cold blood and by skulking in some dark cubbyhole.'

'My dear sir! Nothing, I assure you, could have been further from my thoughts,' said Holmes.

Davenport subsided, somewhat mollified. 'I apologize, sir,' said he. 'But this dreadful business has been eating at me like the worm i' the bud, as someone once remarked.'

'Then you will understand that the sooner we can clear it up, the better?'

Davenport nodded. 'Fire away!'

'Can you think of anyone in the place with any reason to kill Morgan?'

'No, sir, and I could swear to that on oath. Even Peter Gregson, although there was some inexplicable antipathy between them, never seemed to hate Ben, they just did not get on well together. Indeed, I would defy anyone to dislike Ben; you might differ with some of his opinions, but you could not help but like the man.'

'Thank you.'

'Was there anything else?' Davenport asked. 'I think a breath of fresh air would do me good at the moment.'

'There was nothing else just now.'

Davenport got up, nodded to us, and left the room. Holmes studied the *Strand* for a moment, then threw it back on the shelf. 'Well?' said he.

'This artistic temperament seems to excuse much,' said I.

'One might have one's doubts, but it is a well-known phenomenon. Many of the great artists have led less than conventional lives ... Cellini, for example.'

'Yes. And that fellow who cut off his own ear.'

'But he was a Dutchman, Holmes!'

'Ah, that explains it, then. And ...' Holmes broke off as the door opened, and Jeremy Lane came into the library.

Seven

'I did not know anyone was in here,' Lane said, pausing in the doorway.

Holmes waved a hand at the chairs, as Davenport had done earlier. 'Please sit down,' said he. 'I should be grateful for your help with a few small problems.'

Lane sat down, looking somewhat apprehensive. 'Of course, if there is anything I can do to help ...' said he. 'Although I fear ...'

'It is merely a small thing,' said Holmes. 'You were, you said, asleep in here when Gregson found the body?'

'That is so. I woke up when they all came in here, Tomlinson and Pountney, I mean, bringing Gregson with them. I woke up then, all right, for he was still making a dreadful din!'

'Yes, I am told that Gregson's response to finding the body was somewhat dramatic. So noisy, in fact, that it brought Tomlinson from the sitting room, and even drew Pountney downstairs from his bedroom. I have known men who slept soundly, I allow ... indeed, Watson takes some waking ... but even so I find it curious that you should sleep through such an alarm.'

Lane stared at the book-lined shelves. 'Indeed. And, as I believe I have already said, I am very mindful of the fact that, had I been awake, I might have prevented the tragedy, or at the very least identified the guilty party.'

'Well, we cannot be certain as to that. After all, there were others in the house. Welsh was next door in the kitchen when the murder took place, Tomlinson was in the sitting room, and neither of them seems to have seen or heard anything which might have prevented, or avenged, the crime,' said Holmes. He waited, and when Lane said nothing, he added gently, 'On the other hand, they both heard Gregson when he found the body. So, you will understand that I am curious as to why you did not awaken?'

'Oh, yes.' Lane looked embarrassed. 'The fact is ... look here, Mr Holmes, everyone knows you, and Dr Watson here. But have you ever actually heard of Jeremy Lane? Before you were summoned here, that is?'

'As Watson will tell you, my knowledge of literature is of the scantiest.'

'And you, Doctor? You are yourself a man of letters, after all?' Lane asked me.

'I am a busy man, sir! I have not as much time as I should wish to keep up with today's vast outpourings of literary works by all and sundry,' said I stiffly.

Lane laughed aloud. 'Well said, Doctor! But, sir, I can assure you that had you all the time in the world, were you to subscribe to every periodical now being published, you would be hard put to it to know the name of Jeremy Lane. Oh, I have published one or two small pieces, delicate gems of poetry and prose ... who has not? But ...' and here he broke off and glanced at the door, which was closed – 'you will please to treat this as strictly between ourselves? The fact is, my first post after leaving college was in a City firm. I had a taste for writing, and ... as I thought ... some small talent. A modest legacy some three years ago prompted me to chuck the job in and try writing. I soon realized that my small talent was small indeed, or so editors and publishers seem to think. Things have gone badly ... damned badly, to be brutally frank ... and the modest legacy is now well-nigh exhausted. I came down here partly by way of an intermission from the constant worry about what is to become of me, and partly to see if I could not drum up some new ideas. I have been sleeping poorly of late, and even the country air did not seem to help much. Yesterday I had a headache, with lack of sleep, perhaps, so I came in here and took a dose of laudanum. It got rid of the headache by the simple, but effective, expedient of putting me to sleep almost at once, and I knew nothing more until the party came in here, and all the racket started.'

'Ah,' said Holmes, 'that quite explains it. Thank you. I am sorry your efforts have not met with the rewards which I am certain they deserve, but perhaps that will change in the near future?'

'It is kind of you to say so,' said Lane, 'but I fear you are being overly optimistic.' He stood up. 'I think perhaps a turn in the grounds might clear my head.'

'You are still not sleeping?' said I.

Lane shook his head.

'Well,' I told him, 'laudanum is indeed effective, but I would not recommend its repeated use. I have seen too many men ... aye, and women, too ... become addicted to the stuff.'

'I shall abjure it forthwith,' said Lane, with some of his old cynicism, as he left the room.

When Lane had gone, Holmes turned to me. 'Would laudanum account for his not hearing Gregson?' he asked.

'Oh, yes, if the dose were large enough.'

'So, we are to envisage Lane coming in here and taking a dose of laudanum because he had been suffering from insomnia ...' Holmes frowned. 'But then why did he not simply go upstairs and take to his bed, I wonder?'

'Perhaps he was not being quite honest with us?' I suggested. 'He did say that his Muse had deserted him ... perhaps the truth is that he sought inspiration in the opiate, like de Quincey, or the "Ancient Mariner" fellow, Coleridge, was it?'

'H'mm, that is certainly possible. Seeking his Muse in his drug-induced dreams. Dreams, I wonder ... or nightmares? How say you to that notion, friend Watson?'

'What, a nightmare? Killing Morgan under the impression that he was fighting some hideous phantasm? I suppose it is possible,' said I doubtfully, 'and I could not entirely rule it out, for I have known opium cause some odd hallucinations. But opium dreams are usually not accompanied by any great bodily activity ... the dreamer remains in his chair, or on his bed. So, the effect would be unusual, in my experience. With bhang, the hashish of the Arabs, perhaps, or that noisome Devil's Foot Root we came across, but not the poppy, not as a rule.'

'I bow to your greater knowledge of drugs.' Holmes looked at his watch. 'It is almost the hour for afternoon tea, so we might as well stay in here.'

As he had said, it was not long before Mrs Welsh came in with the customary trays, cups and saucers, and what have you. I was not sorry to see a large cake on one plate, for I had not eaten since breakfast, and I fear that I have not Holmes's single-mindedness of purpose. The other guests were not long in arriving, and Morrison introduced Holmes to those he had not yet had a chance to meet.

The atmosphere was somewhat strained, I must confess, but perhaps that was only to be expected, under the circumstances. Holmes did his best to put the others at their ease, and with some success. I was delighted to see that he also found time to eat some bread and butter, and two portions of cake, for I had feared that he might be starving himself in order – as he would put it – that his reasoning powers might be the keener.

I noticed further that Holmes approached Gregson, and had a quiet word with him. I could not guess what had been said, but when tea was over and there was a general move out of the library, Gregson remained behind, and when only the three of us were left, he said, 'Here I am, Mr Holmes. What was so secret that it could not be said sooner?'

'Nothing secret, not as such. Merely a few points requiring clarification. Did you ever find your lost palette knife, by the by?'

Gregson shook his head. 'I have not really looked for it, not properly. Other, and more pressing, matters have obtruded in an uncivil way, demanding my attention. I fear the palette knife is gone for ever. But, since the murder was not committed with it, it hardly seems important, does it?'

'Hardly. When you came in from the garden, you closed the outer door behind you?'

'I closed it, but did not lock it.'

'And when Morgan went into the porch from the dining room, did he close the inner door?'

'Yes, I saw it close as I left the dining room. He would naturally not wish to be overheard.'

'Indeed not. Now, as you left the dining room to go to the front door, did you see or hear anyone else?'

Gregson shook his head. 'There was nobody about, Mr Holmes, I can swear to that.'

'There could not possibly have been anyone concealed on the stairs, let us say?'

Another shake of the head answered him. 'I cannot believe so.'

'Would you just run through the events of yesterday afternoon once more, to be certain?'

Gregson pulled a face, and sighed theatrically.

'I know that it is difficult, and tiresome, and unsettling,' said Holmes, 'but I assure you that it is important.'

'Very well. I tried to telephone Sarah just after luncheon ... say two o'clock or just before. There was no answer. I went outside ... I had already set up a small easel, and intended to do some painting or sketching. I tried to settle to that, without much success. I had been out there for some time, when Welsh and his assistant walked past me, and Welsh said, I think, "Time for tea", something like that, and the assistant said, "A warm day", as I recall. I had not realized it was so late ... I had meant to try the telephone again and it was odd that I should have left it so long. I looked at my watch, made some remark about the lateness of the hour, how time flies, something quite trite of that kind, and said that I would try the telephone, if I recall correctly.' He broke off, and asked, 'Is this truly necessary?'

'Your account is most detailed, and may be of the greatest use.'

'If you say so. I came into the house ...'

113

'One moment,' said Holmes. 'You are certain there was no-one in the garden?'

'Sure as eggs is eggs. Welsh and his lad will tell you the same. The whole place was deserted. In fact, I have seldom known it so quiet, for on a warm day there is usually someone else around the garden. The air was hot, as you know, yesterday, still almost to the point of being oppressive. Even the birds seemed exhausted by the heat, and had grown tired of singing. It may all sound very poetic, but it is literally true. I am certain I should have known had anyone come into the garden.'

'And the house was similarly quiet?'

'It was.'

'I suppose you would not have noticed anyone looking out of a window, say?'

'Oh, yes,' said Gregson unexpectedly. 'I was sketching the house, you see.'

'Oh?'

'It is not my usual sort of subject, I must confess. I favour the more modern school. But the old place looked so quiet and peaceful ... just like a sepia plate in a popular magazine, with some trite caption ... "Does dear old England slumber still?" ... that kind of drivel. I could not concentrate on anything more complicated by way of a subject, and so I did a rather rapid but nevertheless elegant sketch of the place. I will swear that there was no-one at any of the windows whilst I was out there working, Mr Holmes.'

'And when you came inside?'

Gregson paused. 'Well, of course, then I put my sketch aside.'

'And would not have particularly noticed anyone looking out of a window?'

'Probably not. No, not then.'

'And when Morgan came into the dining room, and you left to smoke a cigarette at the front door, you are certain there was nobody else in the house, so far as you could tell?'

'Quite certain. I have told you that I could swear to that. The house was empty, at least downstairs.'

'You see,' said Holmes in his gentlest tones, 'the problem which faces Watson and myself is just this ... you might well have been seen entering the porch from the garden, but having once closed the outer door, you could not be seen leaving the porch. Nor could anyone in the garden have seen Morgan going in. And you have just said that you would swear that no-one inside the house saw you leave the dining room. Presumably, then, no-one inside the house would have seen Morgan go in.' And he put his hands together, and sunk his head on to them.

'I do not ...' Gregson hesitated. He thought about it for a long moment, then said, 'Good Lord! Are you suggesting that it was I, and not Morgan, whom the murderer planned to kill?'

'Well, that would certainly be one theory,' said Holmes.

'But ... Still,' said Gregson thoughtfully, 'it would make a damned sight more sense. After all ... well ...' and he lapsed into silence.

'Have you reason to believe that anyone here wished to see you dead?' asked Holmes.

'Good Lord, no!'

'You know most of the other guests here quite well?'

'Most of them. I've known James Davenport for years, and Pountney and Tomlinson as well. I first met Morrison when he became secretary, three, or possibly four, years ago.'

'And Lane? Had you met him before?'

'I met him only last week, this is his first visit.'

'And you have no dark secrets in your past that might account for any animosity?'

'Oh, dozens. Hundreds. But no Jeremy Lanes among 'em, thank Heaven!'

'And yet you said that it made more sense? More sense to think that the murderer was planning to kill you, than that he planned to kill Morgan? Is that what you meant?'

'Well.' Gregson gave a sort of shamefaced laugh. 'I was only thinking that there are probably more people here with reason to ... to dislike me, than there are who disliked Ben. That was all.'

'And again, would you like to be more specific?'

Gregson sat in silence for a while. 'No, sir,' said he at last with what seemed a sudden access of resolution, 'quite frankly, I should not. I will not deny that I have had some small differences of opinion with others who are staying in the house, but there is, I am certain, nothing that would have caused any of them to wish me dead ... or at least, to wish for it so badly that they would attempt to hasten the process. I would insult them ... and myself ... if I thought as much.' He hesitated. 'Tell me,' he added, 'do you really believe that I am in some sort of danger?'

'It is certainly a possibility, if indeed you were the murderer's intended victim,' said Holmes. 'However, we may be able to mitigate the danger to some extent. We ... Watson and I ... shall keep an eye on you until dinner this evening.'

'And thereafter?'

Holmes smiled. 'I shall not spoil the surprise.' His face grew serious again. 'But I must ask you to trust me implicitly. Whatever happens ... however grave it may seem, however startling ... you must not lose hope, but have confidence that everything is for the best. Can you do that, think you?'

'It is a little awkward, without knowing just what you have in mind for me,' said Gregson. 'But, yes ... I believe that I can put a brave face on it.'

'Well said!' and Holmes shook Gregson's hand vigorously.

'I think I may go up to my room,' said Gregson.

I half-rose. 'Shall I ...'

Gregson smiled. 'I hardly think it necessary, Doctor. I shall be very careful. And I shall lock my door, you may be certain of that.'

I glanced at Holmes, but he waved me to my chair. 'We shall call for you towards the dinner hour,' he told Gregson. 'Meantime, although I would not wish to over-state the possible danger, or to alarm you unnecessarily in any way, I should keep my door bolted, as you say, until we do call for you.'

Gregson, looking rather worried and nervous, nodded without speaking, and left the room.

'Holmes,' said I, 'Gregson's remark about someone disliking him, and it's making more sense if they'd tried to kill him … I recall that Tomlinson said much the same sort of thing …' and I broke off as there was a tremendous crash from the hallway.

Holmes leapt to his feet and dashed outside. I followed, and was horrified to see Gregson huddled all in a heap at the foot of the stairs.

Eight

Holmes reached Gregson before I did. It was immediately obvious that the great clatter that we had heard had been caused by the umbrella stand's being knocked over, for it lay on its side, along with a great heap of sticks, on the floor beside Gregson. But I could see that Gregson himself was already starting to get unsteadily to his feet, and there was no sign of any blood, so that I had no immediate fears for his life.

Holmes had evidently reached much the same conclusions as I had. 'Quick, Watson! The front door!' said he. 'Observe, if you have never observed before, but do nothing, and say nothing ... only return and tell me what you see.'

I rushed at once to the heavy front door, opened it, and went outside. There was no-one in the front garden but Morrison, staring gloomily at the plants, and occasionally lashing out at the lawn with his stick.

'Hullo!' said he, as I went outside. 'Having a breath of fresh air? Me too! I am stifled inside, I confess. Not so much lack of air as lack of occupation, or perhaps lack of any apparent end to this dark business.'

Mindful of Holmes's admonition, I said only, 'That gardener fellow ... Evans, is it? ... he is not here, then?'

Morrison's gloom deepened noticeably. 'I sent him off home,' he said shortly.

This was something out of the ordinary; Holmes would not, I was sure, have let it go without further inquiry. 'Indeed?' said I.

119

'Indeed. He had the nerve to turn up here at well after two, and plainly the worse for drink! When I very properly admonished him, he told me that some damn fool ... only Evans said "kind gentleman" ... had given him money to drink his health!'

'I see!' Secretly delighted, but still wanting to help the investigation, I asked, 'Quiet out here, is it not?'

'I find it very restful,' said Morrison pointedly.

'Nobody else been this way at all lately?'

Morrison regarded me with some suspicion. 'No. Why do you ask?'

'Oh, no reason. Just making conversation, that was all. Well, I shall see you later, no doubt,' and I left him staring after me, and returned to the hallway.

Holmes and Gregson were still there, and Mrs Welsh – evidently alarmed by the noise – had joined them. 'Mr Gregson unfortunately tripped over the umbrella stand,' Holmes was telling her as I approached, 'but there is, as you see, no great harm done. Dr Watson will confirm that.'

I had a hasty glance at Gregson's head, but could see no sign of any injury. 'There seems nothing serious, certainly,' I said.

Mrs Welsh sniffed in a disapproving manner. 'Well, sir, if you say so. I'll just set the sticks back ...'

'No, no!' said Holmes quickly. 'You have, I am sure, more than enough work in the kitchen at this hour. Dr Watson will arrange them all in orderly rows ... as Virgil so deftly puts it ... not merely that their vistas may charm a frivolous mind, but so that no-one else will have a similar accident. Sticks are something of a hobby of his, is that not so, Doctor?'

'Oh, indeed. Absolutely. Fascinated by 'em, from being a boy,' said I, wondering vaguely what the devil he was driving at.

'And meantime, I shall take Mr Gregson into the library, so that he may rest and recover somewhat before dinner,' Holmes went on, 'and Dr Watson will join us as soon as he may, and check more thoroughly that all is well.'

I suspect that Mrs Welsh felt something of the same bewilderment that I did, for she stared after Holmes as he escorted Gregson back to the library. Then, prompted doubtless by Holmes's mention of dinner, and thoughts of preparations for the meal still to be carried out, she too disappeared through the kitchen door.

Holmes had evidently intended me to study the distribution of the sticks carefully, and I did so accordingly, but I must confess that I was none the wiser. The stand had been pushed over when Gregson fell against it, that much was obvious, and the sticks had spilled out. Only one, the same great ash plant that I had borrowed earlier, lay a little apart, in the nook formed by the staircase and the kitchen wall.

Still without the least idea of what I was to observe, I set the stand upright again, and replaced the sticks in it, before returning to the library.

'Just take a closer look at his head, would you, Watson?' Holmes asked as I went in.

I examined Gregson's head more carefully than I had done a moment before. 'No, it is just as I thought. No break in the skin, not even any bruising that I can see.'

'I took the worst of the blow on my arm,' Gregson told me. 'It merely glanced off my head. I was dazed for a moment, but not seriously injured, as you can see.'

'Oh? Then I had better see the arm as well. No,' I said, as he rolled up his sleeve, 'nothing to speak of there, either.'

'It hurts like the very devil!' said Gregson. 'It seemed as if he were using a huge club.'

'It was a formidable weapon,' said I. 'I borrowed it … that is, I noticed it … the other day. Well, you may find that a bruise will appear on your arm later, and perhaps your head, but nothing is broken, and no great damage seems apparent.' I straightened up. 'Holmes, if I might have a word with you?'

'In a moment, Doctor. This is surely more pressing. What exactly happened?' Holmes asked Gregson.

'I was on my way upstairs, as you know. I had reached the bottom of the staircase, when I heard some noise in the angle formed by the stair and the wall of the servants' quarters. I started to look in there, and someone struck me with that stick.'

'Where was he standing?'

'He must have been behind me, or to the side. I was suddenly aware of his presence, and I threw up my arm to ward off the blow, but the force of it sent me flying into the umbrella stand.'

'And your assailant made off?'

'Obviously!'

'You did not see who ...'

Gregson shook his head.

'He must have moved fast!' said I.

'Indeed, he must,' said Holmes thoughtfully.

Gregson cleared his throat delicately. 'It rather looks as if you were right, Mr Holmes,' said he.

Holmes did not reply, but went over to the window and looked out. 'We had best accompany you to your room, when you are ready, that is,' said he at last.

We remained in the library for a while – Holmes busy with his own inward thoughts, and Gregson rubbing his head and staring moodily out of the window. I did wonder at Holmes's reaction, but I have learned over the years not to be surprised at anything he does, so after one or two attempts at general conversation – which were rebuffed rather curtly – I picked up the *Strand* which Holmes had thrown back on the shelf, and was soon absorbed in its pages.

When the hour was sufficiently advanced to think of changing for dinner, we went upstairs together in a little party. Holmes and I left Gregson at his door, but we stayed until we heard his bolt go across, and then set off down the corridor.

Holmes's room was somewhat further along the corridor than mine, and as we reached my door he said, 'I should be grateful for a private word, Watson.'

'I rather thought you might,' and I ushered him in, and waved him to a chair.

Holmes filled his pipe, and threw his tobacco pouch over to me. 'What think you to the attack on friend Gregson?' he asked me. 'Is it not a strange coincidence, Doctor? Fancy his being set upon like that so soon after we had warned him.'

'Coincidence be damned!' said I. 'The whole thing was stage-managed.'

'What!' said Holmes in mock surprise, 'you do not mean that he arranged it himself to corroborate our theory that he was the intended victim?'

'Of course, he did! Had he been hit with that ash plant, he'd have known about it all right! There was no sign of any injury at all, Holmes!'

Holmes clapped his hands in admiration. 'Well done, Watson! I confess, the suddenness of it threw me for the moment ... I did not expect anything so audacious.'

'Like a respectable clergyman in your railway compartment, who suddenly starts doing conjuring tricks?'

Holmes laughed, and set a match to his pipe. 'That was why I asked you to look outside. For a moment I genuinely thought that there might have been an attacker, and of course he could not have gone through the kitchen, as Mrs Welsh and the cook were in there. He must needs have gone through the front door, or be hiding in the cloakroom. I sent you to see what you might see in the garden, while I made a point of staying in the hallway with Gregson, so that the exit from the cloakroom was blocked.'

'By the way, Holmes, Morrison ...'

'But I can at least boast that a very hasty second glance aroused my suspicions. If Gregson had been attacked from the front, by someone hiding in the angle of stair and wall, Gregson could not fail to see and identify his assailant. What is more, an assailant in there would have been trapped by Gregson's inert form, and the litter of sticks.'

'Ah, but then he might have clambered over the obstruction?'

'True,' said Holmes, 'but that would have delayed him. We were, I think, pretty quick off the mark when we heard the noise, Watson ... I was certain we should have seen anyone who had been lurking in the corner.'

'But Gregson said the attack came from behind, that is to say, it was committed by someone in the hallway.'

'I knew that he would say that before he did say it! He could hardly say that he had been face to face with his attacker, but not seen him, now could he? And I knew it was untrue ... you saw for yourself that the sticks had been knocked over so that they all pointed into the house. Now, the stand was far enough into the angle of wall and stair to mean that it could only be knocked over that way by someone falling back out of that corner. And I knew that was not the case, as I have explained.'

'It was a bold deduction, Holmes! A man who has been hit by a heavy stick does not look round to see which way he will fall! He might have staggered against the banister, hit the wall, and thus sent the sticks flying?'

'He might,' said Holmes with another laugh, 'I suppose he might, but then he would be lying pointing in the same direction, as it were. Gregson was not ... his head was pointing into the angle of the stair. In other words, he had fallen one way, and the umbrella stand the other. Again, it may have happened that way in a rough-and-tumble attack, but it was the cumulative effect which told against it. It was, as you say, too much like a stage set ... why, I tell you, Watson, I half expected the director to come prancing across the hallway and call out, "No, no, dear boy, I want much more *drama* in it!" As a last point, why did the supposed attacker not finish the job with a well-placed blow of the stick as Gregson lay helpless? Instead, he threw the stick into the angle of the wall! Ridiculous!'

'He might have been confused by the racket and not thinking?'

'Oh, come, Watson! After taking the enormous risk of attacking Gregson in broad daylight, with the house full? And then, where was this attacker just before the attack? Not on the stair, nor yet in the hallway, or Gregson must have seen him there! He was not in the kitchen, or the servants would have seen him. He might have been lurking in the downstairs cloakroom, or by the front door, but then he must needs have moved across the hallway ... which is on a generous scale ... with a turn of speed that would have attracted the attention of the most unobservant!

'And again, what noise in the angle of the wall made Gregson look in there, if the attacker were behind him? And finally, ... and perhaps most telling ... where were the injuries one might expect from such an assault? That "formidable weapon", that "great club", should surely have left one or two small bruises evident even to my layman's eye! His hair was not even disarranged ... he takes a pride in it, and you noted, by the by, that he colours it, very discreetly? No? He does. Then there was no pallor, his breathing was regular, no sign that he was even shaken by the supposed attack, much less injured! It did not fool me, much less a qualified doctor!'

'I did not suspect, until I examined him,' said I.

'But when you did, it did not take you very long to reach the correct conclusion, did it? Fancy his having the nerve to try to fool us like that, Watson! No, I may have been unsettled initially, but I soon saw that the whole thing was patently a fake. He threw the ash plant into the corner with his right hand, at the same time knocking the stand over ... backwards ... with his left, and stretched out alongside the sticks ... not among them, you observed, no doubt, he was careful not to hurt himself ... in a leisurely and gentlemanly fashion.'

'"So that scurrility may have no nourishment", as it were?'

'The quoting of classical and medieval tags ... even in translation ... is symptomatic either of the successful conclusion of a case, or of bewilderment,' said Holmes. 'Since it is not the first, the trained logician would unhesitatingly conclude that it must thus be the second. Are we bewildered, Watson?'

'Slightly, Holmes. The only point of such a deception would be to attempt to show that your theory is correct, and that Gregson was the murderer's intended victim. And the only logical reason for Gregson's wanting to prove the theory correct would be that it was not!' said I. 'And why should Gregson want us to think that Morgan was killed by mistake, so to speak, if he were not ... unless Gregson himself really were the murderer?'

'You sum it up in your inimitable fashion, Watson,' said Holmes. 'Why on earth should he try to fool us in so obvious a fashion? We had already pretty well accepted that it was Gregson's death the murderer planned, and told him as much ... if he is guilty, and he wanted to fool us, he had succeeded, or almost. Why then this very clumsy attempt to push us towards a conclusion we had already reached, when a child could see that it must have the opposite effect?'

'Over-egging the pudding, as it were? Criminals do stupid things, though, Holmes. Grow over-confident, think the investigators are fools. After all, if Gregson did kill Morgan, then he has already taken a very dangerous course by drawing attention to his finding ... or apparently finding ... the body in the dramatic way that he did. It might be part and parcel of the same melodramatic character. He may simply be unable to help himself, to stop himself over-dramatizing.'

'You are right, Watson. Criminals do stupid things.' And he repeated slowly, 'Criminals do stupid things. But then ...' He shook his head, and got up. 'For all that, I am far from satisfied, Doctor. If Gregson ...' and he shook his head again. 'Still,' he added with a sudden quiet chuckle, 'I think that possibility too may be covered by my plans for later this evening.' And, before I could ask what those plans might be, he had nodded a farewell and left my room.

I washed and changed, and waited for Holmes to call for me. Together we collected Gregson, who was silent and seemingly deep in thought, and we all three went downstairs.

The mood at dinner was still not what it would have been under happier circumstances, but the others seemed relieved by Holmes's presence, reassured that the mystery might soon be resolved. For his part, Holmes regaled the company with tales of our early exploits together – but I noticed that he carefully avoided mentioning any cases which involved murder, violence or sudden death. The meal went off, in short, far better than I had feared, and the evening passed quickly enough.

We had taken our coffee and cigars into the library, and the evening was fairly well advanced, when our relative tranquillity was disturbed by a ring at the front door. We looked at one another, wondering who it might be, until Mrs Welsh entered the room. She looked round, then spoke to Morrison. 'It's the police, sir,' said she. 'Inspector Forrester would like a word with you.'

Morrison, a worried look on his face, went out, to return a moment later. 'I rather fear they want to talk to you, Gregson,' he said.

Gregson raised an eyebrow, but said nothing. He got up and left the room, and Holmes quickly followed him, closing the door behind him.

We could hear the inspector's voice, though the words could not be made out, then Gregson said something, then Holmes's rather penetrating voice – 'Now, remember!' – and then Gregson again said something, still indistinct. Then the front door banged shut, and Holmes came back into the library, alone.

There was a moment's silence. 'Well?' said I, for it was clear that the others were too timid, or too polite, to ask what had happened.

'Inspector Forrester has taken Gregson into custody,' said Holmes, rubbing his hands with every indication of delight, though his face showed no emotion whatever.

Nine

I realized at once that this was Holmes's doing, the result of his telephone call earlier that afternoon. The others, of course, did not realize it, and there was a moment's pause, then everyone began to speak at once. When the din had eventually subsided somewhat, Morrison demanded, 'They have really arrested him, then?'

'So it would seem,' said Holmes.

'They must think him guilty, then!' said Pountney.

And Tomlinson muttered, 'Told you so!' to the room at large.

'Well!' said Davenport. 'I feel sorry for poor old Peter, but if he is guilty ... well! And at any rate,' he added in a shamefaced sort of way, 'it does mean that the rest of us are no longer under that dreadful cloud of suspicion.'

'It does indeed,' said Morrison, consulting his watch. He stood up. 'And, that being so, I will ask you to excuse me ... I shall return home tonight, before it is quite dark. I shall be back tomorrow, of course.' He left the room, and we heard the front door open and close again.

'Well, Mr Holmes,' said Davenport, 'if this is your doing, then you have my most sincere thanks, sir.'

The rest of them expressed similar sentiments, but Holmes made no reply, beyond a smile or bow of the head. There was an almost palpable air of relief about the room, as though the storm had at last broken, and the intolerably oppressive atmosphere had given way to something which was at least recognizable, albeit still a touch unpleasant. The others all appeared to accept that Gregson had indeed killed Morgan, though only Tomlinson went so far as to say as much, and there was some inconclusive speculation as to the reason for the murder. Again, Holmes made only non-committal replies to the many questions that were very naturally addressed to him, and the conversation soon grew more general.

Whilst the others were discussing something or other, I took the opportunity to take Holmes on one side and ask him if Gregson's 'arrest' were indeed his doing. He laughed in his peculiar silent fashion. 'It was, Watson. We are safe either way, you see, for if he is innocent, and in danger, then ... although his bed may be harder, and his tomorrow's breakfast scantier, than he might have wished ... at least he is safe where he is, for the moment.'

'And if he is guilty, you get the credit for a speedy arrest!'

'Well, at any rate Forrester does. But I own, Watson, that I am still far from happy ... despite his inept performance earlier today.'

'You think he may yet be innocent?'

'Let us say that further enquiries may not come amiss. Fortunately, we have already taken much of our testimony, and this evening's almost festive mood may make our task easier still.'

Ten minutes or so later, Lane announced that he was off to bed. There seemed to be a general inclination to follow his example, but Holmes said, 'I wonder if Watson and myself might have a few moments with you, Mr Pountney, and you, Mr Tomlinson?'

They looked at him in some surprise, and with perhaps a touch of resentment at the prospect of their slumbers being delayed, but agreed readily enough. Davenport, who also seemed surprised at the request, excused himself, and the four of us were left in sole possession of the library.

'Well, Mr Holmes?' said Tomlinson. 'I had hoped the whole sad and sordid business would be concluded with tonight's news.'

'Hardly that, sir!' said Holmes. 'There is sure to be a sensational trial, with the guests ... such as yourself ... being called to testify.'

'Lord, yes!' said Pountney, gloomily. 'Never thought of that. He's right, of course, Henry, there's sure to be a good deal of public interest in the case.'

'That is, always assuming that Gregson comes to trial,' said Holmes carefully.

'And why on earth should he not?' asked Tomlinson, staring at him.

'Well, for the very simple reason that it is by no means certain that the case against him will stand up in court.'

Tomlinson and Pountney looked at him in silence for a moment, then Tomlinson gave a dismissive snort. 'And why should it not, sir? It was his letter opener which committed the crime; he was found at the scene. What more is necessary, pray?'

'What was the reason for the crime?' asked Holmes gently.

'Well, that is easy enough! We all knew they did not get on!' said Tomlinson.

But Pountney, in a more reasoned tone, said, 'Come, Henry! We all fail to "get on" with someone, do we not? It is not in human nature to like everyone, after all. But we do not kill everyone we take a dislike to.'

'Then who did kill Morgan?' demanded Tomlinson. 'If, as you say, Gregson's dislike of the man was insufficient reason ... and I am not disposed to argue that point too vigorously now ... then none among the rest of us had even that trifling cause for murder!'

'I had thought,' said Holmes, 'that if you were to go over the events of yesterday once more, with Watson and myself, something might perhaps emerge ... something you had overlooked earlier as being of no importance, say?'

Tomlinson gave a theatrical sigh. 'The police have already asked us the selfsame thing,' said he.

'True,' said Holmes, 'but you were very naturally upset yesterday, and may thus have failed to mention some detail ...

some apparently trivial detail, as I say … which may yet prove not so trivial after all.'

Tomlinson shook his head, and made to stand up.

'Come, sir!' said Holmes. 'You would not have an innocent man go to the gallows, merely because it would keep you out of bed for half an hour? Think of the lifetime of sleepless nights that would result!'

'He is right, Henry,' said Pountney. 'And then, think of the dinner invitations that one would receive, were one to be instrumental in bringing the real murderer to book! Come, sir,' he said to Holmes, 'ask your questions. I shall answer for Henry's good behaviour.'

Tomlinson threw up his hands in mock resignation. 'I probably should not have been able to sleep anyway, with all the excitement of today's events,' said he. 'Dick is right … fire away, Mr Holmes, and we shall answer you.'

'I am very glad to hear you say so,' said Holmes, 'for I am certain you must know much about the place, and the people in it, which Watson and I, as outsiders, could never hope to guess at. Now, the first and most obvious question must be, who had any reason to kill Morgan?'

Tomlinson shook his head. 'No-one! I have said as much already!'

Pountney said, 'Henry puts it baldly, but he is right, Mr Holmes. As he said a moment ago, if we allow that Gregson had no reason to kill Ben Morgan, then nobody else in the place had a reason either. I can truthfully say that everyone got on well with him.'

'And yet someone stabbed him to death!'

'It is indeed a mystery,' said Tomlinson.

'You are right,' said Holmes. 'Mr Pountney, may I begin with you?'

Pountney looked apprehensive, but nodded agreement.

'At the time of the murder, you were upstairs, I think?'

'I was,' said Pountney. 'I had luncheon with the others, and then I went up to my room to write some letters … nothing of any great moment, just notes to some old friends to whom I had been meaning to write for the past week. We all know which road is paved with good intentions, I think! Well, I had intended to catch up on my correspondence as soon as the weather became inclement, and kept me inside, but of course it has been perfect ... glorious summer days the whole time. Yesterday, I determined that despite the heat I would at last get them written, and set to work accordingly.'

'I have seen Morgan's room,' said Holmes, 'and Watson's, and my own, of course, and all three have a substantial table under the window. Has yours the same?'

Pountney nodded. 'All the rooms are alike in that regard.'

'And you sat at the table to write your letters?'

'I did.'

'From where you were seated, could you see out over the garden?'

Pountney thought a moment. 'It rather depends. If you are busy writing, you bend over the table, and thus cannot be said to be looking at the garden. I was pretty much doing that, I believe. Of course, if you straighten up, you might well stare out for inspiration, as it were.'

'And did you straighten up and stare out for inspiration?' asked Holmes.

'Oh, very likely. One does, I find.'

'And on these occasions, you sought inspiration ... where? In the garden itself, or in the distant views over the countryside?'

'Hard to say,' said Pountney vaguely. 'One looks without really seeing, as it were.'

'"You see, but you do not observe", perhaps?' I asked.

Holmes gave me a stern look, but Pountney only nodded, and said, 'That is it, exactly!'

'But you may have looked at the garden?' Holmes went on.

'I may well have done so. I simply cannot say with any degree of truth whether or not I did so,' said Pountney. 'However, I can truthfully say that if I did look at the garden, I should have noticed anything at all out of the way. I was not so absorbed in what I was doing as to miss any excitement, I can assure you!'

'You do not recall seeing Gregson sketching out there, say? Or Welsh about his duties in the rose beds?'

'No, I cannot say that I marked either of them. But then, one gets used to seeing Welsh and his fellows out there at all times of the day, so that if I had seen him, it may well not have made any great impression upon my mind. Peter? No, again I cannot recall seeing him particularly. But then, if he were sitting on the bench at the kitchen side of the garden, as I believe he was, then I most likely would be unable to see him from where I was sitting ... I should have had to stand up and move closer to the window in order to command a view of that side.'

'H'mm. Now,' said Holmes, 'I understand that Gregson was very upset when he found the body?'

'You can say that again!' said Tomlinson, with a short laugh. 'If, indeed, he did find it, and that too was not merely a counterfeit.'

'If you please,' said Holmes. 'I shall come to you in a moment. Now, Mr Pountney, when did you first realize that something was wrong? When you heard Gregson in the dining room?'

'Yes. I became aware of a noise, it sounded like a hammering ... I think Peter must have pounded on the kitchen door, to attract Welsh's attention, call for help, that sort of thing. Of course, I did not at first know that it was Peter ... I could not recognize the voice, much less could I make out any words ... but the noise attracted my attention. To be honest with you, my first thought was that it was some tramp, or drunk, who had wandered into the house, and was being ejected by Welsh and his men.' He hesitated. 'I confess that I did not immediately rush to investigate ... oh, there was a time when I would have been first on the scene all right, but age makes a man cautious. Then I rebuked myself for my pusillanimity, and set off down the stairs. I reached the bend in the staircase, and could see Welsh standing in the doorway of the dining room, his arm round Peter, as if to support him. Well, naturally I went down right away to see if I could help. Henry got to the door at about the same time, did you not?'

'Yes,' said Tomlinson, 'I heard the racket, just as Dick did, and ...'

Holmes stopped him again. 'All in good time,' said he. And to Pountney, 'Pray continue.'

'There's really not too much more to add. Welsh said that Ben had been hurt, and I assumed there had been some sort of accident at first. Welsh asked if Henry and I could see to Peter, and summon Gordon Morrison. We took Peter into the library ... Lane was in there, fast asleep ...'

'Lazy young devil!' grunted Tomlinson.

'I stayed with Peter, and tried to calm him down a bit. And Henry went for Morrison. That's more or less the end of the story. Peter did calm down a bit, Lane woke up, and Henry came back and into the library to see what was happening. Peter told his tale, in a very disjointed and incoherent sort of fashion ... I have to confess I simply could not believe him, not at first. I thought he was making it up, some sort of a bizarre joke, perhaps, despite his obvious distress. Then Morrison came in and said he had sent for the police, and he confirmed Peter's story, said that Ben had been stabbed to death. My mind still could not accept it, but then the police arrived, and of course I realized it must be true, difficult though it was to believe.'

'Thank you,' said Holmes. 'And you, Mr Tomlinson?'

'I cannot add much to Dick's account. I was in the sitting room, working, when I heard the noise along the corridor.'

'Working?'

'I compose, a little,' said Tomlinson, rather self-consciously.

'Indeed? For the piano, or the violin, perhaps?'

'I am working on a full orchestral symphony, at the moment.'

'That is an ambitious enterprise,' said Holmes admiringly.

'It is, sir,' said Tomlinson. 'Far beyond my usual small efforts. And, because of that, I wanted some peace and quiet, that I might collate what I have done thus far. I took my bits and pieces into the sitting room, and set to work.'

'You did not notice anything unusual in the house, or in the garden?'

135

'No, sir. But then, like Dick here, I was busy, and I cannot say that I broke off from my work to look outside particularly.'

'You worked without any interruptions?'

'Yes, until that racket started.'

'What did you think it was?'

'I'm damned if I know,' said Tomlinson. 'I could not make out just what it was, I only know that I wished it would stop. Then I decided to take a look, as it sounded so odd. I came along the corridor, and ... as Dick says ... I saw Welsh and Gregson at the dining room door. I think Dick and I more or less got there together. I went upstairs to fetch Gordon, and we took a look at poor Ben's body. It was glaringly obvious that medical aid would be useless, so Gordon asked Welsh to keep an eye on the dining room, and sent for the police. As Dick has told you, I went into the library to see what was going on. And things happened after that just as he said.'

'Thank you, that is very clear,' said Holmes. 'There are just one or two points on which I would ask for clarification. First of all, you are sure that Lane was asleep when you first entered the library with Gregson?'

'Oh, yes,' said Pountney, and Tomlinson confirmed it with a grunted vilification of all lazy young devils.

'You see,' said Holmes, 'I find it odd that the noise which Gregson made should have brought you two, in one case from the other end of the corridor, and in the other from upstairs, and yet it did not disturb Lane's slumbers?'

'He seemed well and truly in the Land of Nod,' said Tomlinson. 'It was not until we barged in here that he showed any signs of stirring. I agree it seems strange but I have no explanation to offer, I'm afraid.'

'No,' said Holmes. 'Did either of you happen to notice whether the windows in here were open when you brought Gregson in?'

'They were,' said Tomlinson. 'Or at least, they were open a bit later. I know that because Peter was lighting one cigarette after another ... to steady his nerves, I expect ... and the air got a bit thick, so I looked at the window, intending to open it, but someone already had.'

'Not I,' said Pountney, 'and I did not see anyone else open it, so it must have been open when we first went in. Lane most likely opened it when he went for his forty winks.'

'Idle hound!' said Tomlinson. 'He vanished, of course, when the row started in here ... I didn't see him again until an hour or so later, when he was wandering about with that damned notebook of his. You know, I rather think he is enjoying all this fuss. Mind you, I must say that I never have been able to get on with literary men ... present company excepted, of course, Doctor! Most of 'em are too clever by half, for my taste. Or at any rate, they think they are.'

'And they are forever cadging drinks and cigarettes,' added Pountney rather offensively.

'Really, sir!' said I.

'Well, then,' said Holmes with a laugh, 'what of the secretary? You, Pountney, were upstairs, and yet still you heard Gregson; while Morrison was upstairs, and did not.'

'Ah, but my room is right at the top of the staircase,' Pountney said, 'and my door was open. I may have been indoors, but I did not want to stifle with the heat, and so I opened both door and window to let some air into the room. Moreover, the stairwell acts as a sort of sounding board, or echo chamber. You can hear quite low conversations in the hall as you come down the stairs ... not that one listens, of course,' he added hastily, 'but one cannot help noticing.'

Tomlinson nodded. 'That's true,' he said, 'I've noticed that myself. And, of course, Gordon's room is right at the other end of the upstairs corridor. And I know that his door was closed, for I knocked at it when I went to fetch him. And he was using his typewriting machine, for I heard the keys clattering as I reached the door. I suppose that, taken all together, those circumstances would explain his not having heard the noise.'

'Indeed. You, Mr Pountney, did not think to call for the secretary before you came downstairs to investigate the upset?' asked Holmes.

'Never occurred to me. But then, it was Tuesday, you see, and Gordon does not usually come to the house on Tuesdays, just Mondays and Fridays. And then with his room being at the other end of the corridor ... I suppose that at the time I just did not recall that he was in the house.'

'No. Well, this does all confirm what we have already found out,' said Holmes.

'So, it was all a waste of time after all!' said Tomlinson.

'By no means, sir. It is quite essential that the investigator confirms his data from as many independent sources as possible. Now, if I may impose just a little more upon your patience ... according to Watson here, you, Mr Tomlinson, made some remark to the effect that you might have understood it better had the murderer attempted to kill Gregson, or words to that effect. And Gregson himself has hinted much the same to me. I must ask you, sir, if you would explain what you meant?'

Tomlinson looked at him for a long moment, then he stood up. 'No, sir,' said he with a surprising forcefulness for a man of his years, 'I shall not explain! I'm damned if I will!' He turned from Holmes, and stared at me in open contempt. 'And as for this business of sneaking, of reporting what one may have overheard in a private conversation, I might excuse it in the midst of a murder investigation, despicable though it is at the best of times. But, since the police have arrested the man whom I consider to be the self-evident culprit, I cannot see that you have any further cause to ask these personal questions, and I shall certainly not answer them!' And with that, he nodded to Pountney, and stormed out.

Pountney looked after him. Then he looked unhappily from Holmes to me and back again, and said, 'Oh, dear!'

Ten

'Oh, dear!' said Pountney again.

'Now, sir,' said Holmes, 'you must see that Mr Tomlinson's response was not such as to convince Dr Watson and myself that he is entirely free from suspicion in this matter. It would, perhaps, be as well if you were to tell us what you know.'

Pountney looked unhappily from Holmes to me, and back again. As if to gain time to consider his reply, he took an old briar pipe from his pocket and stared at it. Holmes threw his tobacco pouch to him. 'Thank you, sir,' said Pountney, filling his pipe. 'You must not mind Henry,' he added. 'He only flared up in that way because he is upset. He'll feel bad about it later, and apologize handsomely, I am certain of that. Come to that, this business of poor Ben's being killed is enough to unsettle anyone. Under ordinary circumstances, Henry would never have dreamed of speaking to you in that uncivil fashion. He is the most easy-going of men, as a general rule.'

'I do not dispute it,' said Holmes. 'But I have to tell you, sir, that Dr Watson and I are by no means convinced that the police have the right man in custody.'

Pountney paused in the act of lighting his pipe, and stared at Holmes until the match burned down to his finger and he gave a little start and blew it out. 'Like Henry, I had assumed that the matter was resolved,' said he, lighting another match.

Holmes shook his head. 'There are some puzzling aspects to the case.'

'Such as Peter's not having the slightest reason to kill Ben, you mean?' said Pountney quickly.

'That, and other circumstances.'

'I must confess that it did bother me,' said Pountney with a more sympathetic air than he had hitherto shown. 'Yes. It seemed so ... so very pointless.'

'Indeed. So, you will agree with me that it is most desirable that we should clear the matter up properly? It is no more than our duty, after all. A duty we owe both to Mr Gregson, for if he is innocent, then he should be released; and no less to poor Mr Morgan, whose death should be avenged. And, for good measure, it is very necessary that the true murderer be caught, for who can say but that he might not kill again?'

'Good Lord! That's true enough!' said Pountney. He hesitated. 'And what if ... I cannot believe it, mind you, but it is possible ... what if Peter Gregson is guilty after all?'

'Then we have done no harm. And we may even establish a reason for his committing the crime.'

Pountney shrugged his shoulders. 'If you really think it may help. Though I must say that I agree with Henry that idle gossip is unlikely to solve the mystery.'

'Idle gossip, as you call it, is very often the detective's greatest ally,' said Holmes. 'Now, this remark which Tomlinson made about his understanding it if someone had killed Gregson ... he must have had something specific in mind, I think, to make him say that.'

Pountney shrugged his shoulders, but said nothing. Holmes waited, also without speaking. At last, Pountney mumbled, 'It was all a long time ago, now. I should like to help, of course, but I really cannot see that it could be relevant.'

'You and Tomlinson have known each other many years, I gather?' said Holmes.

'Oh, yes.' Pountney seemed relieved at this apparent change of subject. 'From our school days, in point of fact. Then we studied music together, even shared diggings in London, waiting for fame and fortune to come along.' He laughed. 'They never did, of course, or not to any notable degree. But we did pretty well.'

'And the friendship has obviously lasted?'

'As you can see. When Henry married, of course, he moved out ... they took a house out Islington way. I visited them there several times, and enjoyed the place so much that I vowed that when I retired, I should move there. I did, too ... I have a little house in the same road as Henry. Very pleasant.'

'And Tomlinson's wife has no objections to his coming here and leaving her alone?' asked Holmes.

'Oh, she is not with him any more,' said Pountney vaguely, putting another match to his pipe, which had gone out. Holmes did not say anything, and when Pountney had his pipe lit to his satisfaction, he went on unprompted, 'We are both on our own, now, Henry and I, so naturally we see a good deal of one another ... quite like our bachelor days, in fact. I never married, and have no close family, and Henry is in the same boat, these days.'

'You said that his wife had died?' said Holmes.

'I did not say that.' Pountney paused. 'Although she did, in point of fact.' He smoked in silence for a while.

Again, Holmes said nothing, but began to fill his own pipe.

At last, Pountney said, 'Look here, Mr Holmes, as I told you at the start, I do not approve of gossip, not as such. But you have a reputation for discretion ... and you, Doctor, I rely on you to hide names and places and so on pretty thoroughly. And so, if it will help solve this mystery, I shall tell you. But this is not widely known, and I shall be grateful if it might stay that way.'

'You may rely on us,' said Holmes.

'Very well, then. As you could see, old Henry is not exactly fond of Peter. It goes back a while ... a good while. Twenty years, in point of fact.' He sighed, perhaps musing on the inexorable passage of Time's winged chariot. 'It is said that if a man commits no indiscretions at twenty, he will commit them at forty. Not that it was an indiscretion, of course, very far from it! But Henry was forty, more than forty, and he met a younger woman. Considerably younger, in fact. She came to him for lessons, that's how it started. She was a brilliant musician in her own right, and could have built a considerable reputation, with

141

time and the proper opportunities. And she was attractive.' He put another match to his pipe, although it did not seem strictly necessary. 'Yes, a good deal younger.' He paused, then shook himself. 'But that did not matter. Not at all.'

'They married, I take it?' said Holmes.

Pountney nodded. 'The age difference, as I say, did not matter. I'll swear to that. No, the trouble was, you see, that she was ... what can I call it? ... emotional. Sensitive. Too damned sensitive, if you ask me, like so many people associated with what are so preciously called "The Arts". She seemed to need continual reassurance about her work, needed to be told that it was good. You understand? Peter is much the same, perhaps you noticed?'

Holmes nodded, but did not interrupt.

'Henry was doing well in those days,' Pountney went on. 'A brilliant violinist. Could have had a national reputation ... international. Easily. Could have ... and should have. He had tremendous confidence in himself, too. Knew he was good. Brimming with self-confidence, knew he couldn't put a foot wrong.' He sighed. 'That was the trouble, you see. He had so much confidence that he just could not see that his wife was the other way, didn't realize that she needed this constant praise. I do not criticize him, you are to understand ... I merely point out that such was the case.

'Well, Henry got the chance to tour on the Continent ... Paris, Berlin, Prague. A wonderful opportunity, naturally, and a great honour. He might have been able to take his wife with him, too, it could have been arranged somehow. But, as ill-luck would have it, she too had secured a long engagement, in London. So, she had to stay behind.' He played at lighting his pipe again.

'And?' said Holmes.

Pountney shrugged his shoulders. 'The usual thing, I'm afraid. Henry was off on his Continental tour. His wife fell into one of her melancholic moods.' He sighed. 'I wish to Heaven she had come to me! But ... I suppose she thought of me as Henry's friend, did not see me ... anyway, she did not. And Peter, you see ... he knew them both, though not well, and ...

well, I'm sure you understand. I think he very likely understood how she felt, being prone to those same black moods himself. I think that was all he had intended, to lend a sympathetic ear. As it was, of course ...' and he broke off, and shrugged again.

'You have obviously known Gregson a long time as well, then?'

'Twenty years? Thirty? One loses count. There is a distinct art world, and a music world, of course, more or less closed to outsiders, but whose inhabitants all know one another. Understandable ... after all, one would not be surprised if the good Doctor here knew a dozen other medical men, would one?'

'I suppose not,' said Holmes. 'You were saying ...'

'Oh, that. Not much more to tell, really. It could not be kept quiet, of course ... not in that small circle. And Henry ... although he is tolerant enough as a general rule ... he has his own ideas, his own standards.'

'He divorced her?'

Pountney nodded. 'He did. I think that she had expected that Peter would "do the decent thing", as the saying goes, "make an honest woman of her". But Peter simply did not see it in that light. As far as he was concerned, what had happened was by mutual agreement, and that was an end of it. Enjoyable enough ... at least, I trust it was, or the fuss was all for nothing ... but without any sort of obligation on his part. It is not that he is evil, or immoral. He simply sees things a little differently from the majority of us, that is all. I have to say that I never blamed Peter. Never blamed him at all. He did the right thing, by his own lights. He could not see that the lady might see things in another light.' He smoked his pipe in silence.

'And that was the cause of Tomlinson's remark?' Holmes asked.

'More or less.' Pountney shrugged his shoulders. There was a long pause, then he went on, 'The story did not end there. What with the divorce, and then Peter's desertion of her ... what she saw as his desertion of her, although even I cannot honestly lay any blame at his door, as I say ... and then being

143

prey to melancholia ... to cut a long story short, she took her own life.'

'Good Heavens!' said I.

Pountney nodded. 'It was a tremendous shock. I was horrified, and of course Henry was absolutely ... well, you may imagine. I do not think he had ever ceased to love her, you see, despite everything. And then of course he blamed Peter for the whole business. Wrongly, unjustifiably, in my view. But you cannot blame Henry for thinking like that, can you? And Henry has never really forgiven Peter. So, you see, Mr Holmes, that if it had been Peter who had been killed, and not Ben Morgan, then Henry might indeed have been a suspect.'

'You see,' said Holmes gently, 'the difficulty lies in this ... anyone might have seen Gregson go into the porch from the garden, but it would be well-nigh impossible for anyone to see him leave, and Morgan take his place. You do see what that implies, do you not?'

'Not in the least,' said Pountney. He frowned. 'Stop a moment, though. Are you suggesting that the murderer intended to kill not Morgan, but Gregson?'

'It is a possibility.'

Pountney whistled. 'And that is why you were asking about Henry? I see!' Incredibly, he smiled. 'But in that event, Mr Holmes, you have not one suspect, but two.'

'Indeed? And who is the second, pray?'

'It is none other than myself!' said Pountney. 'And I have a good deal better cause to kill Peter than has Henry.'

Holmes raised an eyebrow.

'There is one last twist in my tale,' Pountney went on. 'I should not have told you this, had it not been for your silly notion about Henry, because it is nobody's business but my own. But, since you do entertain that silly notion, I shall tell you what I have never told another living soul. I have said that I never married. That was not particularly from choice, nor because I have no inclinations in that direction ... unlike a lot of the fellows one meets in this "Art" world! No, I did meet a woman I could have loved, could have married. Only Henry met her first. "One of life's little ironies", is the cliché that comes to mind. She had eyes for nobody but Henry, so of course I could never say anything. And when they married ... well, I wished them every happiness, and I meant it. Oh, I cannot pretend that there was never the odd twinge of regret, but, what with knowing and liking Henry for so long, and so well, and ... and her ... well, I wished them every happiness.' He paused. 'She knew, of course. They always do. Perhaps that is why she did not come to me, when Henry was away. Perhaps she felt easier talking to Peter, on the grounds that he was not involved. Who can say? Another little irony, if it were so!'

'But then, after the divorce ...' said Holmes, gently.

'I cannot tell you, sir. Perhaps my feelings had changed? Remember, if you will, that I saw the whole thing mainly from Henry's point of view. He confided in me, and I felt his sense of betrayal, of horror, at what had been done to him. And then ... being as I am a touch old-fashioned myself ... I perhaps expected Peter to offer her his hand and his name. Despite the fact that I knew him so well. And then of course there was the sheer difficulty of making my own feelings known. What could I have said? "Madam, my best, my oldest friend has just divorced you, so will you have dinner with me?" It hardly rings true, does it? I suppose some men might ... these days, of course ... well! But I know I could not. And, by the time I had collected my thoughts, it was too late.'

Holmes leaned over, and put a hand on his shoulder. 'I am truly sorry, sir,' he said gently. 'Both for what happened, and for prying into so delicate a subject.'

'Oh, it doesn't matter,' said Pountney. 'Not now. Not after all this time. Time may bring new troubles, but it also heals the old ones, even the very worst of them. But my real point was that although Henry suffered once, I suffered twice. Not merely because of what happened to the lady concerned, but because of what happened to Henry. His own career went to the devil, while I watched. He still loved her, you see. He took refuge in the bottle, for a time. I got him to a doctor, helped him with that, stopped it before it got too bad. But by that time, he had lost his name for reliability, for brilliance. His laboriously won reputation was gone, and he never recovered it. Nor wanted to.

Oh, he scratched a living, he was never a poor man, nothing like that. But the glory, the praise he should have had, that never came. So, if Henry is a suspect, then I am as well, because by my reckoning, I have twice as many reasons to kill Peter as Henry has. And, just in case you were wondering, I'm damned sure that I did not kill Ben by mistake for Peter!' And with that, he stood up, bade us good night civilly enough, and left the room.

'Well, Watson?' Holmes asked me.

'A tragic tale, Holmes!' I shook my head, and patted my pockets.

Holmes laughed, and threw me his cigarette case. 'Pountney was right about one attribute of literary men.'

'Nonsense, Holmes! Run out of cigarettes temporarily, nothing more! Yes, a tragic business. But, tragic though it is, it is yesterday's news. To kill this week for something done twenty years ago? It does not ring true, to paraphrase Mr Pountney.'

'It could not have festered over the decades? You recall that business at Norwood, do you not?'

'The lunatic who brooded over the fact that the woman he loved had married another man, you mean? Tried to take his revenge on her son after twenty years? Yes, I recall it, Holmes. You do not think this is another such case?'

Holmes shook his head. 'I do not think so. But who can say? You recollect that Oldacre attempted to fake his own murder, to implicate the lad.'

'And there is a parallel with the use of Gregson's letter opener, you mean? To implicate him?'

'Well, it is an interesting possibility, is it not? But I am inclined to dismiss it as being, as you say, yesterday's news. In the Norwood case, Oldacre waited until the son should be old enough to hang for the supposed murder. But there is nothing of that kind here, so why should Tomlinson wait so long to revenge himself on Gregson? Why not act at the time?' He shook his head again. 'For all that, one thing which does emerge is Gregson's womanizing, and its tragic consequences. That has been a recurring theme, Watson, and it must be investigated further ... not for some affair twenty years ago, but in case there is anything more recent. And, since Mrs Welsh is the only woman in the house whom Gregson might have approached, I fear that ... indelicate though it may be ... we must have a talk with her.'

'In that case, for Heaven's sake let me ask the questions!' said I hastily.

'Yes, the fair sex has always been your department! You may be sure that I shall be as discreet as possible.' Holmes consulted his watch. 'I suppose it is too late to think of seeing Mrs Welsh now.'

'Far too late,' said I.

'You are right,' said Holmes. But he said it reluctantly, and I am sure that, had I not been there, the Welshes' sleep would have been disturbed that night.

Eleven

The following day, Holmes lingered over his breakfast in a fashion that was most uncharacteristic when he was engaged upon a case – though it was a different story when he was not! This circumstance was much to my secret amusement, for I knew well enough what he was about. Sure enough, when all the others had left the dining room, and Mrs Welsh looked in, he said, 'Ah, Mrs Welsh! We have quite finished, thank you.'

Mrs Welsh gave him a dazzling smile, and began to clear the table.

'Watson rose somewhat late, I fear, but I am not entirely displeased that his loafing has kept us here,' said Holmes rather mendaciously, 'for I wanted the opportunity of a word with you.'

'Indeed, sir?'

'Indeed. Pray take a seat.'

Mrs Welsh looked somewhat apprehensive at this. 'Well, sir ...'

'It will be quite in order, I assure you,' said Holmes. For a man who has always shown himself quite immune to the charms of women, Holmes has a most persuasive way with the fair sex when he so chooses, and Mrs Welsh sat down without further demur.

'This sad business must have quite unsettled the ordered life of the house,' Holmes began.

Mrs Welsh pursed her lips. 'Indeed, it has, Mr Holmes. Unsettling ... yes, sir, that is just the word for it.'

'And I imagine that running a large, old place of this kind, more or less single-handed, is enough of a task at the best of times?'

'Oh, it's not so bad, sir, not in the general run of things. You get into your little routines, as it were, to help things run smoothly.'

'Indeed. Tell me,' said Holmes, 'is there ... that is to say, I could imagine that things might occasionally be somewhat ... embarrassing, shall I say? ... given the nature of the place.'

I groaned inwardly at this colossal ineptitude, but Mrs Welsh was too puzzled to be offended. 'I am not sure I follow you, Mr Holmes.'

'Well, is it not sometimes awkward ... a whole house full of men, and yourself the only attractive ... I may say, very attractive ... woman?'

'You are forgetting Elsie and Doris, the maids, sir,' said Mrs Welsh. But she flushed as she said it, and patted her hair in a becoming fashion.

'Ah, yes,' said Holmes. 'But ... delightful though they indubitably are ... they are here only throughout the day.'

'Well, I won't deny that some of the guests ... and especially the older gentlemen ... do have a way with them,' said Mrs Welsh. 'But usually it shows as little courtesies, or what you might call gallantry. If there were anything else ... well, I'm sure I can look after myself.'

'Indeed, you can!' said I heartily. 'And I must say, Holmes, that I never ...'

Holmes held up a hand. 'Bear with me, Doctor! Now, Mrs Welsh, Watson here has a theory that Mr Gregson did not commit the murder.'

'Well, sir, I could have told you that!' said Mrs Welsh. 'He's such a nice, quiet gentleman. Oh, I don't say that even he doesn't have a way with him, sometimes. But murder? Never! Begging your pardon, sir.'

'But you see, in order to clear his name, we must make some rather personal enquiries,' Holmes went on.

'Yes, sir, I can see that. But I assure you that there was nothing of that sort. Not here. I am given to understand that Mr Gregson is what I believe is generally called a "ladies' man", but he was never anything other than the soul of courtesy to me,' said Mrs Welsh with just a touch of iciness in her demeanour. 'Now, if you gentlemen will excuse me?' And she stood up, and went on with clearing the table.

'Thank you,' said Holmes. 'I am sorry if I have offended you. But I had entertained hopes that we might have cleared Mr Gregson's name.'

Mrs Welsh paused in her work. 'And these questions might have helped with that?'

'I had hoped as much.'

'Well ...' Mrs Welsh hesitated. 'It isn't my place to gossip, sir.'

'Indeed not.'

'And it is only gossip, as far as I know. But ... well, you might have a word with the rector.'

'The rector?'

'I'm saying no more,' said Mrs Welsh firmly, as she left for the kitchen.

'Right, Watson! Do you know where the rectory might be?'

'Well, at least I know where the church is, which is evidently more than you do! And I presume the rectory is not far from there.'

'Lead on, Doctor.'

I led the way down the lane, all aglow in the morning sunlight, until we reached the little old church. The rectory stood at no great distance, and we were soon turning into the drive through a gate bearing a brass plate that read 'The Rev. Dr Obadiah Montfort, DD'.

'Curious!' said I.

Holmes looked at me.

'The rector's name,' said I. 'It ...' and I stopped, as a middle-aged clergyman, evidently Dr Montfort himself, appeared on the steps.

'Good morning, sir!' said Holmes cheerily. 'Have I the honour of addressing Dr Montfort?'

'You have, sir.' The rector looked from Holmes to me.

Holmes handed over his card. 'My name is Sherlock Holmes, and this is Doctor John Watson.'

The rector raised an eyebrow. 'Indeed? Your name is not totally unfamiliar to me, sir, although I must confess that I had not hitherto believed in your existence.'

'Oh?'

The rector laughed. 'I have read Dr Watson's stories in a rather lurid magazine, more than one copy of which I have had occasion to confiscate from errant choirboys,' said he. 'It is a surprise ... albeit a pleasant one ... to find that you are as real as I am.'

Holmes laughed with him. 'Oh, Watson and I are real enough,' said he.

'Come inside,' said the rector, and led the way to a little sitting room furnished in what I should have called a bachelor's taste. 'My wife refuses to allow me to smoke in the main rooms,' he said by way of explanation, 'so please ... make yourselves at home.' And he took an ancient briar from the mantelshelf, and patted his pockets in an absent-minded fashion.

Holmes sighed, threw his tobacco pouch to the rector, scribbled a note on his shirt cuff – I leaned over and read: 'Bradleys 2lb shag' – and said, 'We are here about this sad business over at Belmont.'

The rector frowned. 'I heard something of it,' said he. 'I was not consulted in any spiritual capacity, you are to understand, but heard it merely as servants' gossip. I sincerely trust that I am free from what our forefathers might have called "enthusiasm" ... I do not draw any parallels between the world of "Art" and "Letters" and those Cities of the Plain whose names cause so much innocent amusement to the village lads in our Bible classes. Yet for all that, I could wish that some of the guests down the road would devote a little less of their time and energy to the things of this world. It might save a good deal of distress in the long run.'

'Amen to that!' said Holmes. 'You and I, sir, are not entirely dissimilar in that we are too often consulted as a last resort, when it is too late for that word of good advice which might have saved the day.'

The rector nodded. 'True enough. But, in a more practical vein, I cannot see that I can shed any light on the matter. As I say, anything I have heard has been at second ... or, rather, third ... hand.'

'It is drawing a bow at a venture, I know,' said Holmes. 'But I have reason to think that you have had dealings with Belmont ... or, rather, with one or more of the guests there ... which may have some bearing on the present problem.'

The rector's brow clouded. He smoked in silence for a time before saying, 'It is a painful subject for me, sir. I know you cannot have known that, but it is so. I must therefore ask you to excuse my not discussing the matter. On any other head, you may rely on my responding as fully as I may.'

Holmes seemed at a loss. To break the silence that ensued, I asked, 'I was struck by your name, Dr Montfort. You are not by any chance related to the chief constable, Colonel de Montfort?'

The rector's brow cleared at once. 'He is by way of being a distant cousin of mine,' said he. He waved a hand to indicate a shelf which held a long row of great scrapbooks. 'I am something of an amateur of genealogy,' he went on, 'and could show you the exact relationship, were you interested, but it would take some time. It is my ambition eventually to prove a connection between my own humble family and those de Montforts, father and son, whose names are ... or at least, should be ... familiar to every schoolboy.'

'But you have not yet succeeded in that?' I asked.

'Alas! No.'

'Colonel de Montfort is an acquaintance of mine,' said I. 'In point of fact, it was he who asked Mr Holmes to look into the business at Belmont.'

'Oh!' said the rector. 'That puts a slightly different complexion on things, of course. I would wish to help if I could, but yet ...'

'You may have the utmost confidence in our discretion,' said Holmes. 'Watson has already promised as much to the chief constable, and to the secretary at Belmont.'

153

'Very well, I rely on you. It was my ward, Miss Sarah Pollit,' said the rector. 'The only daughter of one of my oldest and closest college friends. He and his wife died tragically in an epidemic of cholera, almost twenty years back, and Sarah came to live with us. She was a good girl, though somewhat headstrong, and she had a definite talent for drawing and painting. When she came into her father's money at the age of twenty-one, she determined to make a career of art, and accordingly she sought out the inhabitants of Belmont.'

'She could not stay there, though, under the terms of the trust,' said I.

'No, Doctor, but she could ... and did ... make the acquaintance of the secretary's wife, Mrs Morrison. And then it was but a simple matter to obtain an introduction to some of the guests. One, in particular.' He sighed.

'Peter Gregson?' asked Holmes.

The rector nodded. 'He undertook to give her lessons ... oh, it was all correct enough, he came here and I, or my wife, acted as chaperon. But, as men of the world, you will be well enough aware that there are subtler forms of seduction than the obvious ... the man was a good talker, and discourse of crowds, of bright lights, of gaiety ... these things must have their effect on the young and impressionable mind.'

'Do I understand you to say that there was some understanding, some liaison, between Gregson and your ward?' asked Holmes.

'I do not say so,' said the rector. 'I do not ... I cannot ... believe that. But Sarah determined that she would pursue her career by moving to London. She had control of her own money by then, so I had no say in that. All I could do was give my advice, and that I did ... but it was ignored. Now, I am not one of those who would see London as all that is bad, as some sink of iniquity, but I could none the less wish that she had not gone. Or, having gone, that she was a little older and wiser, or perhaps a little less rich and attractive ... for she is both. I am most concerned about her, Mr Holmes.'

'You are right to be, sir. Have you kept in touch with her?'

'I have her address, and I have many times taken up my pen to write to her, but something prevented me. To repeat my advice would be supererogatory, and possibly even seem presumptuous ... and yet I cannot with any good conscience applaud her actions.'

'But you would answer if she wrote? You would not turn her away if she paid you a visit?'

'Indeed not! Nothing could please me more, or my wife ... or my daughter, who looks upon Sarah not as a friend but as a sister. Indeed, my daughter is engaged to be married, and I know that she wants nothing more than for Sarah to be present and act as a bridesmaid.'

'May I have a note of her address?' asked Holmes. 'I think your Miss Pollit may perhaps throw some light on this matter at Belmont, and there are some questions I would wish to ask her. At the same time ... but only if you wish it ... I could pass on your remarks as to wanting to see her, and so forth.'

'I should esteem it a great kindness if you would,' said the rector, scribbling on a piece of paper. 'Please assure her of our unswerving affection, and say that any word from her will have a loving and immediate response.'

'It is a pleasure to hear you say so, sir,' said Holmes warmly, shaking the rector's hand. 'And now, we must take our leave.'

The rector showed us out, and Holmes set off at a good pace in the direction of the little railway halt. 'We can enquire about local trains at the inn,' said he, 'and hire a trap if we are unlucky.'

'You think this Miss Sarah Pollit will shed some light on the matter?'

'It is possible. In any event, it is the most up-to-date line of enquiry we have encountered thus far!' said Holmes, laughing.

We were lucky with the trains – as Holmes almost invariably was – and towards the hour of luncheon we alighted at Victoria.

Twelve

We took a cab at Victoria, and were soon rattling along Cheyne Walk, which has been home to so many famous men of letters and the arts. The cab turned into a less well-known street, and drew up before a house built in the reign of Queen Anne.

'There is the studio,' said Holmes, nodding up to where half the roof had been taken off and replaced by a huge skylight. 'It is not a recent conversion. I wonder who has owned the place over the years? Some of these old London houses could tell a tale or two, if they could but speak!'

He rang the bell, and the door was opened by an elderly maid of a most respectable – if not downright terrifying – appearance. Holmes handed over our cards, and said, 'Might we speak to Miss Sarah Pollit?'

The maid looked at him suspiciously, and I was beginning to doubt whether we should be admitted, when an attractive young woman of twenty-two or -three appeared in the corridor behind the maid and asked, 'Who is it, Violet?'

The maid gave a shrug, and passed our cards to the young woman.

'Mr Sherlock Holmes? And Dr Watson? Please come in, gentlemen. Violet,' she said to the maid, 'please bring us some tea.'

She led the way to a small but comfortable sitting room, and showed us to chairs.

'Miss Sarah Pollit, I take it?' said Holmes.

'Yes. I'm sorry, I was forgetting the social niceties. You must ascribe that to my excitement at the fact that Mr Holmes and Dr Watson have called upon me. It is not every day that that happens, of course. But I am intrigued ... what on earth can the renowned Mr Holmes of Baker Street possibly want with me?'

'We spoke with the Reverend Dr Montfort this morning,' said Holmes.

Miss Pollit's jaw set in a determined fashion. 'He does not want you to take me back there, does he? Because if so, I can tell you ...'

Holmes held up a hand. 'Nothing of that kind, I can assure you, madam. Dr Montfort did, however, ask me to pass his compliments and kind wishes on to you, and to assure you that his door will always be open to you.'

Miss Pollit clapped her hands, and laughed aloud. 'Oh, he is a darling! As are you for bringing me the news! That is to say,' she added hastily, 'I am most grateful to you, sir. I did not wish to quarrel with Uncle Obadiah ... I call him "uncle", although he is not, of course ... indeed, there was no real quarrel, but I know that he was desperately unhappy when I left. As was I, in some sense. Oh, thank you, Violet,' she said, as the maid brought in a tray, and set it down with somewhat of a disapproving look at Holmes and myself.

'Your "uncle", as you call him, the rector, I should say, is most concerned for your welfare,' said Holmes.

'I can appreciate that,' said Miss Pollit. 'But, really, he has little to fear, Mr Holmes. I am not entirely foolish, and you can see for yourself that Violet ... though she has the kindest of hearts ... presents something of the appearance of a dragon. I rely on her to keep out any undesirables.'

Holmes laughed. 'Well, I merely pass on the rector's remarks,' said he. 'I was to be especially scrupulous in telling you that he would not wish to lose touch with you altogether.'

Miss Pollit poured the tea, for which I was grateful, as Holmes had not allowed us to pause for any refreshments. 'It was very good of him to do so ... and very good of you to take the trouble to pass on his kind words. But, then,' she asked with a little frown, 'if Uncle Obadiah has not asked you to persuade me to return, what is the purpose of your visit? Or ... I do not mean to be rude ... but is it just a social call?'

'Indeed not,' said Holmes. 'Tell me, are you acquainted with a Mr Benjamin Morgan?'

'No.'

'You are sure?'

'Certain, Mr Holmes. Why do you ask me that?'

'What of a Mr Peter Gregson?'

'Why, yes! I know Mr Gregson. In fact, he was very kind to me when first I decided to move here. He found this place for me, indeed, and I should never have been able to do that for myself. Again, I ask why you want to know these things?'

'It is a rather serious matter, Miss Pollit,' said Holmes. 'Mr Morgan has been murdered ...'

'Murdered! Oh, surely not?'

'And Mr Gregson has been arrested for the crime,' finished Holmes.

'Now, that is ridiculous!'

'I am inclined to agree with you,' said Holmes. 'But in order to establish his innocence, I must ask what might appear to be impertinent questions. May I do so now?'

'Oh, if it will help Mr Gregson, yes! But I really cannot imagine what I might tell you that could help.'

'Well,' said Holmes, choosing his words with some care, 'you said, I think, that when you first moved to London, Mr Gregson was very good to you?'

'Oh, yes! He found me this house, as I told you. And he found dear Violet for me, to keep away what he called "the lounge lizards", by which I think he meant adventurers, and ... and men of that sort. And he introduced me to a good many influential people, gallery owners, art critics, that kind of thing. Influential, and useful to the aspiring artist ... though, frankly, many of them do seem to me to fall very much into the lounge lizard category.'

'And ... forgive me, I mean no offence ... but that was the whole nature of your relationship?'

'I do not ... oh!' said Miss Pollit, flushing. 'I see! No, Mr Holmes, you may take my word for it that there was nothing untoward. Nothing that would bring a frown to Uncle Obadiah's brow. I regarded Mr Gregson ... he asked me to call him "Peter", but that seemed unseemly. Oh, dear! That sounded horrible, did it not? ... I mean that it would have been unseemly, what with him being so much older. Oh, now that sounds worse! He began to call me "Sarah", of course, but that was all right. What was I saying? Yes ... that I regard him rather in the light of the father I had lost. And I think ... does this sound too sickly? ... that he sees me as the daughter he never had.'

'I see,' said Holmes, patently puzzled. 'Have you seen Mr Gregson recently?'

'Not for a couple of months. He used to look in on me every day or so, when I first moved here, to see that I getting along satisfactorily. But then his visits grew less frequent ... not that we grew apart or anything, but he seemed to be more easy in his mind about me, when he saw that there was nothing to worry about. He escorted me to several dances, and glowered at the young men if they ventured on any familiarity! But, no, I have not seen him recently.'

'Well, that does not really help us,' said Holmes, getting to his feet, 'but it does seem to eliminate one possible line of enquiry. I am sorry to have troubled you, Miss Pollit. And I am sorry to have to bring you the sad news about Mr Morgan.'

'Naturally, I am very sorry that the poor man is dead ... who would not be? But, since I did not know him, you can see that it does not grieve me in any deep personal sense. No, I am far more concerned that Mr Gregson should be suspected of so horrid a thing! I only wish I could do more to help him. Could I visit him, do you think?'

Holmes shook his head. 'I do not think that would be a good idea.'

'I owe him so much, you see. I would have been stifled had I stayed in the village. And yet, because I was a girl and not a boy, because I am a woman and not a man, I was not ... I am not ... expected to travel, or to earn my living, or ... or anything.'

'Plenty of women earn their living,' said Holmes with a smile. 'Plenty of them are obliged to, for they have not your advantages.'

'Oh, as governesses, and housekeepers, and that sort of thing. Looking after men, or the children of men. But not as writers, or artists, or anything of that sort. That is all seen as men's work. Why, if I had been a man, who would think it odd if I moved to London and became a painter, or if I went off alone on the Grand Tour ... or its modern equivalent, rather, sowing my wild oats in Paris, or somewhere?'

'Really, Madam!' said I. 'And besides, plenty of ladies have been great travellers.'

'Oh, indeed they have. "The great English eccentrics", is the phrase that comes to mind! Elderly ladies, dressing up in exotic garb and taking young Arab lovers! No, thank you, Doctor!'

'Really!' I said again, at something of a loss for a reply.

Miss Pollit gave a wicked smile. 'Do I shock you? You are not familiar with my work, I take it? No? Well, come along, and you will soon see why I could not paint as I would wish in the dear old rectory.'

She set off upstairs. Holmes looked at me, raised an eyebrow, and followed without comment. I followed him, and Miss Pollit ushered us into her studio.

I looked around the large room, every surface of which was covered with studies of the female form in the costume – or lack thereof – and style that one associates most readily with Alma-Tadema.

'You must use a good deal of pink paint!' said I involuntarily.

'Now,' said Miss Pollit, 'tell me why it should shock you that I paint these subjects? Why is it right for a man to paint like this, and wrong for me to do so?'

'Well ...'

'Well, then, if only men are to paint women like this, should I perhaps paint men in classical poses?'

'Good Lord!' said I. 'Heaven forbid!'

'Come, Doctor,' said Miss Pollit, laughing, 'shall I not paint you in the style of Michelangelo's *David*, do you think?'

161

Confused, I stared at a painting entitled, 'The Marriage of Athena' – although frankly it looked to me more like 'The Rape of the Sabine Women'. Seeking to change the subject, I said, 'By the way, Miss Pollit, Holmes here quite forgot to mention that the rector's daughter is to be married, and you are invited to the wedding, to be a bridesmaid.'

'Oh, how wonderful!'

'And perhaps one day she will be invited to yours?' suggested Holmes.

'Perhaps,' said Miss Pollit. 'Or again,' she added very seriously, 'perhaps I shall stay unmarried, and take a lover when I am forty.'

Holmes laughed. 'Whatever he may be, he will be a very lucky man. Indeed, I am surprised that you have not done anything in that direction already ... or is "dear Violet" perhaps too indiscriminating as to what constitutes a lounge lizard?'

Miss Pollit laughed with him. 'Perhaps so. Although there have been admirers.'

'I could hardly have thought otherwise,' said Holmes.

Miss Pollit's face clouded. 'There was one ... another reason for my wanting to move here. But you would not be interested, I'm sure!'

'On the contrary, I should be most interested,' said Holmes.

'Well, it is the old story ... his feelings for me were sincere, and all that kind of thing, but I simply did not reciprocate them. He was a bit younger than me ... not a serious difference, but I think women grow up quicker than men anyway, do not you? He was very ... what can I call it? ... intense. He wanted marriage, but on his terms, and those terms were that I should have children, and be always busy about the house, and never, ever lift my head to see out of the kitchen window.' She sighed. 'It was a pity, because I liked him, and might have grown to love him ... he was handsome, and intelligent ... far cleverer than I am. And I liked his father, poor man.'

'And his name,' said Holmes dreamily, still looking at the huge canvases, 'was John Merryweather.'

Miss Pollit stared at him. 'How on earth did you know that?'

162

'No matter,' said Holmes. 'Come along, Watson … we must return to Belmont, I fear.'

'Do call a cab, Holmes,' said I. 'I shall join you presently.'

Thirteen

Holmes sat in silence in the cab to Victoria. Thinking to cheer him up, I said, 'Likening me to Michelangelo's *David*, indeed!'

Holmes gave a weak smile, then sank back into his seat, and occupied himself with his own thoughts. I did not venture to disturb him again, and at Victoria he disappeared on some mysterious errand, and left me alone. I took the opportunity to have a sandwich and a glass of beer.

Holmes was equally uncommunicative on the train. It was only as we neared Redhill that he consulted his watch, and said, 'Ten minutes to go!' He sighed. 'Why do these poor wretches carry on in such a fashion, Watson? It is pretty clear what happened, of course. Gregson told us that he had passed the time of day with Welsh and Merryweather at tea time … he very probably said, "I must telephone Sarah", or something of that kind, speaking in an absent-minded manner, and meaning the gallery owner, of course. But Merryweather … who evidently resented Miss Pollit's moving away, and perhaps even saw it as her jilting him … thought that there was some illicit liaison between the girl he had lost and Gregson, whom Merryweather would naturally cast in the role of the elderly roué who had seduced her. It must have sounded as if Gregson were crowing over him, rubbing it in.'

'And this lad killed Morgan by mistake, just as we thought?'

Holmes nodded. 'I telephoned to Inspector Forrester, and he and his men will be at Redhill to meet us.'

'One thing still puzzles me, Holmes.'

'Indeed?'

'How did the lad get the letter opener? He said the gardeners ... Welsh excepted ... never went into the main house.'

'Ah, but we have only his word for that, Watson! Most probably ...' and he broke off, and drummed his fingers on the carriage window.

'It suggests premeditation,' said I. 'And, if your theory is correct, it was not premeditated! After all, he would hardly steal the letter opener on the off-chance that Gregson would sneer at him, now would he?'

Holmes scowled. 'It is a difficulty,' he admitted. 'And I confess that I have no easy answer just yet. We shall have to ask the lad himself.' And he sat back in a gloomy silence once again.

At Redhill we were met by Inspector Forrester, with a sergeant and a couple of constables. Gregson was there, too, none the worse for his incarceration, but looking as puzzled as I admit I felt.

I think that we all had questions to ask Holmes, but as the traps which Forrester had provided clattered along the country lanes, Holmes dismissed all attempts to engage him in conversation. It was not until our little party had stepped down at the gate of Belmont that he said, 'I think we shall restrict it to you, Watson, and you, Inspector. Leave your fellows here for the moment ... I do not expect any trouble.'

'If you say so, Mr Holmes.'

Holmes led the way round the side of the house to the back garden, where Welsh and Merryweather were busy about their day's work.

Welsh looked as we neared him, and was about to give a cheery greeting, but then he saw our faces. 'What's the matter?' he asked anxiously.

'I think it is I they wish to see, Mr Welsh,' said Merryweather quietly. 'I have rather been expecting this, gentlemen,' he added. 'You need have no concern, I shall make no sort of fuss. Only ...' and he looked at the ground.

'You understand that we have no choice?' said Holmes gently.

Merryweather nodded. 'It will kill my father, though,' said he sadly.

'You should have thought of that sooner, sir!' Holmes told him more sternly. 'Does your conscience not trouble you unduly?'

'Not unduly. Oh, I might have acted otherwise ... I wish I had, for that matter. But ... no.'

Holmes looked astounded. 'What, it does not bother you that you killed the wrong man? A man innocent of any crime, save wanting to use the telephone?'

It was now Merryweather who looked astonished. 'What on earth are you raving about?' he asked. 'What do you mean by "the wrong man"?'

Holmes stared at him. 'Do you deny that you meant to kill Gregson, but killed Morgan instead?'

'No! I mean, yes ... I do deny it. Gregson? Why should I want to kill that pompous ass?'

'Because you thought that he had stolen the woman you loved.'

Merryweather shook his head. 'You are either very clever, Mr Holmes, or very stupid. Either way, I fear you have quite lost me.'

'Why, I am speaking of Miss Sarah Pollit!'

'Sarah? Oh, that was ages ago ... a boyish fancy. I am engaged, now ... or at any rate I was, for I doubt if the rector will allow his daughter to marry me at the foot of the scaffold.'

'For God's sake, man!' I burst out. 'Why did you kill Gregson?'

'Why, because he ran off with my mother, of course. Did she not tell you?'

'She is out of the country,' said Holmes gently. 'So, that was it, was it?'

Merryweather nodded. 'It broke my father's heart. Dr Watson here will say that there is no such ailment, but I can testify that there is. If you had seen his face when the black mood of despair is upon him ... why, death itself is preferable to such a life! And he knows it ... many a time I have been obliged to hide his razor, and watch him secretly, lest he harm himself. Monday was such a night. I had no sleep, for I dared not leave him. I should have stayed with him the next day, only he seemed a little better, and Mrs Timms promised to watch him, and send for the doctor if need be. My stomach was upset, all right, with the sheer worry of it all. Then I came here, and saw ... saw him, Morgan, walking about as if he owned the place, drinking his port and smoking his cigar, and all the time my poor father was lying in his darkened room, and might have made away with himself by the time I got back home! Morgan did not recognize me, of course ... I was but a lad when my mother ran off, and here of course we were never introduced ... but I knew him all right, and it ate into my soul!' He wiped his brow. 'It was more than I could bear. But even then, I think I could have borne it, only I saw the knife thing on the bench ...'

Holmes held up a hand. 'The letter opener was upstairs, in Gregson's room,' he said.

'Oh, no! It was on the bench, there ...' he waved a hand – 'with his other paints and things. I picked it up ... I picked it up ... and ... and ...' and the rest was lost in a great sob.

'There is no need to continue,' said Holmes. 'Only one more question, if you will ... you saw Gregson go into the porch, did you not? How, then, did you know that he had left, and that Morgan was there in his stead?'

'I saw them,' said Merryweather simply. 'I was passing the french window with my cup of tea, and I happened to look in. Then I saw the letter opener, or whatever you call it, on the bench ... and ... and that was that.'

'Ah!'

'Was there no blood on your hands, though?' I asked.

Merryweather looked at his hands. 'In a literal sense, you mean?' He shook his head. 'I had been reading an article about finger marks a day or so before, and so I made sure to pick the knife up in my handkerchief. There was some blood on that, of course. I stuck the handkerchief in my pocket ... I was terrified that the police would ask me to turn out my pockets, but they never did. They just asked me if I had seen any strangers about the place, and I said quite truthfully that I had not.'

Holmes looked at Forrester, who looked at his boot toes. 'What became of the handkerchief?'

'Oh, I burned it when I got home.'

'I think, Inspector ...'

'Yes, sir.' Forrester motioned to his sergeant, who came and took Merryweather into the house.

'Bad business, sir,' ventured Welsh, who had been a silent spectator throughout.

'It is, indeed,' said Holmes. 'To Forrester, he said, 'I think a word with Gregson might be in order, Inspector.'

'It might at that, Mr Holmes. Or even two words. And I know just the words, though I won't use them in front of you gentlemen.'

He led the way back to the house, but Gregson, released by the sergeant, came out to meet us. He had recovered some of his old jauntiness, and from somewhere or another he had acquired a cigarette, which he was smoking with evident relish.

'Why did you tell us the letter opener was in your room?' asked Forrester without preamble.

'Ah.' Gregson threw away his cigarette. 'That was silly, I know.'

'I can think of another way to describe it, sir,' said Forrester heavily.

'I know! But, you see ... the thing is ... the thing was ... that is, I hadn't killed Ben. I mean, I knew I had not killed him. But there was nobody around who might have killed him, nobody in the house, or the garden. Nobody at all. No sign of any murderer ... except me. I knew just how it must look. So, what was I to do? I did not immediately see things that way ... before I could properly think it out, I panicked, kicked up a fuss, drew attention to myself. Afterwards, of course, when I was in the library just before you arrived, Inspector, I realized that I should have sneaked away quietly, but it was too late. I knew that it looked bad ... me being there, and my letter opener being used, and above all, no other suspects in the vicinity. So, I thought that if I said that the letter opener was upstairs, insisted

169

on it, swore to it, the police would think it was someone else ... that the murderer was someone else, I mean. Which, of course, it was.'

'Why on earth did you need a letter opener outside in the first place?' asked Holmes.

'Because I had lost my palette knife, of course. I had some vague idea of using the letter opener as an improvised palette knife, but when it came right down to it I did not like to misuse it in that cavalier fashion. I can use a brush, but I prefer the knife, to slap on great slabs of paint, not miserable little dabs.'

'Speaking of miserable little dabs ...' began Inspector Forrester.

Holmes held up a hand. 'Do you not realize, sir,' he asked Gregson, 'that if you had simply told the truth, and said that the letter opener was outside the whole time, we might have eliminated many fruitless lines of enquiry? That, indeed, the correct explanation would have been almost self-evident?'

'Oh, yes! Of course, I see that. Now. But, you see, I did not see it at the time. I told you, I lost my head.'

'And that clumsy attempt to make us think that you were the intended victim?' said I. 'That was part of it, too?'

Gregson nodded, shamefaced. 'You were not fooled by that?'

'We were not, sir,' said Holmes. 'Watson spotted it at once!'

'You see,' said Gregson, 'I hoped that if you thought that I was the intended victim, you would not suspect me, but look for the real murderer.'

'I believe you said something like, "criminals do stupid things", Watson?' said Holmes to me. 'Regrettably, so do innocent men!'

'Do you realize further,' said Forrester to Gregson, 'that it is a very serious matter to obstruct the police in the execution of their duties? If it were up to me ...'

'I think we must have an amnesty there,' said Holmes. 'We were all at fault, I think. Gregson for lying to us, me for taking too much on trust, and you, Inspector, for your lamentable failure to find that bloodstained handkerchief!' He turned to me. 'This will scarcely count as one of my greatest successes, Watson!'

'You cannot say that, Mr Holmes!' said Forrester. 'Why, it had us all fooled!'

'I echo that,' said Gregson. 'There were times when I could have sworn that I felt the rope around my neck! You certainly have my eternal gratitude, sir.' He looked at Forrester. 'And I am truly sorry for my foolishness, Inspector,' said he.

'Well,' said Forrester, 'I suppose there is no great harm done at that.' And he nodded a farewell, and set off for the house.

Holmes consulted his watch. 'Enjoy the rest of your stay, Watson,' said he. 'I can just get a train back to London, I think.'

'Will you not stay?' said Gregson. 'There are some questions I should wish to ask you.'

'Yes, Holmes!' I urged. 'It will do you good.'

Holmes smiled. 'Perhaps I will, at that. A murder in the first two days of your stay bodes well, Watson! Who can say what next week may not bring? Yes, I think I shall stay, after all!'

I shuddered, and followed him inside.

171

Fourteen

I had just finished breakfast when Sherlock Holmes came into the room. He glanced at the telephone – no longer with apprehension, but with anticipation – then his gaze moved to the mantelshelf, where a small, modern sculpture had pride of place. He smiled, half to himself, but then his face fell, and he sat down moodily at the table.

'You are right, Holmes,' said I, endeavouring to emulate those feats with which he had so often astonished me in the past, 'it was indeed an interesting case, but with something of a sad conclusion.'

'Amazing, Watson!' said he, managing a smile. 'You are right, of course.' He grew morose again, and pushed his plate away. 'He will hang, Watson, I am sure of it. Oh, I shall do what I can, you may be sure, but English justice does not recognize the "crime of passion" of our French neighbours. Yes, I fear that he will hang.'

'He did kill a man, Holmes! When all is said and done, many of us have suffered losses, by death or by desertion. But we do not all rush out and stick knives into people!'

Holmes shrugged.

In an attempt to distract him, I said, 'One thing does still puzzle me, though, Holmes. That telephone call which the murdered man did not get around to making ... who was it he wanted to speak to, do you think?'

'We are in the region of pure speculation, there,' said Holmes. 'It was not his lady friend, we know that much, for she was abroad. A business matter, perhaps? Or perhaps he had never used the telephone before, and wanted to call some acquaintance, just for the novelty of using the instrument? Indeed, he may possibly have wanted no more than to study the apparatus close up, to see what all the fuss is about. It is one of those irritating loose ends which you can so easily gloss over in your accounts, but which almost invariably crop up in a case none the less.'

'Yes, I suppose so. Holmes, you really should eat something …' I began, but broke off as there was a loud knock at the street door. 'A client?' I ventured – with an access of hope, for I knew that once the sombre mood was upon Holmes, only work – or worse – would bring him out of it.

'It appears so,' said Holmes, as the little page entered the room. 'A case, is it, Billy?'

'Yessir … a big case, it is. For Dr Watson.'

'Oh. An emergency?' I half-rose from my chair, then subsided as a carter's man followed Billy into the room, carrying a packing case, some three feet square and six inches deep.

'Ah!' said I, taking a shilling from my pocket. 'Thank you! I have been expecting this.'

The carter's man touched his cap, and left. Billy seemed disposed to linger in the hope of seeing what I had received, but I ushered him out.

'If I might borrow your penknife, Holmes?'

Holmes watched with interest as I removed the outer crate, then unwrapped some coarse sacking.

'Well, Holmes? What do you think?' and I held up the picture for his approval. 'I bought it from Miss Pollit, asked her to send it on.'

Holmes averted his eyes.

'An honest study from the life, Holmes!'

'Life in the seraglio, perhaps! You surely cannot intend to hang that in here? Think of Billy … a young, impressionable lad! Think of Mrs Hudson! Think of my digestion!'

'I had thought, Holmes ... my bedroom, perhaps?'

'My dear fellow! Think of the effect it might have on the maids!'

'Yes, indeed! That is to say,' I added hastily, as I wrapped my prize in its sacking once again, 'in that event, I shall just have to keep it in my dispatch box at the bank, and look at it only on special occasions.'

Holmes poured himself a cup of coffee. 'You have ... as always, Watson ... arrived at the correct solution.'

"With five volumes you could fill that gap on that second shelf."
(Sherlock Holmes, *The Empty House*)

So why not complete your collection of murder mysteries from Baker Street Studios?
Available from all good bookshops, or direct from the publisher with free UK postage
& packing. To see full details of all our publications, range of audio books, and
special offers visit www.crime4u.com where you can also join our mailing list.

Baker Street Studios Limited, Endeavour House, 170 Woodland Road,
Sawston, Cambridge CB22 3DX
sales@baker-street-studios.com